STRAWBERRY AND SAGE

AMANDA GALE

for my grandparents

CONTENTS

CHAPTER ONE

JUNE, 1954 - LINSBURY, VERMONT

"*I* cannot pay your toll, my prince, for I am but a poor, lonely peasant. But I can offer you a treasure more valuable than gold. And that treasure is my heart."

From the creeping vines beneath her knees, Abigail pulled a plump red strawberry. She cupped her hands and held it for him. He took it. It was heavy with juice and warm from the sun.

He brought it to his lips and opened his mouth. Abigail reached her hand out, her eyes wide and her face aghast.

"No!" she cried. "That's my heart, silly! Why would you want to eat my heart?"

Gabriel lowered his hand. He closed his fingers around it, feeling its prickles.

They were eight years old, and it was a glorious summer evening. They had been playing at Mrs. Wheeler's house since shortly after sunrise. Mrs. Wheeler was Abigail's grandmother. She was tending to her bountiful garden, periodically glancing over her shoulder to check on the children and to smile at their antics. The children themselves had barely noticed her, so absorbed were they in their games, which turned the backyard into a field of wonders. There was ample space to run around on

1

the grass, and there was a hill for rolling. There was the clothesline and her grandmother's sheets, perfect for hiding. And there were strawberries, sweet strawberries, hundreds of them, it seemed, right beneath their feet by the old cellar door. It was here that they had spent most of their time, spoiling their dinners and frolicking in what Abigail insisted was not a little strawberry patch in a Vermont backyard, but rather, a fairy land.

Gabriel shrugged. "It's just a strawberry," he said.

"Gabriel Kelly, you can be such a stick in the mud. We're pretending. Can't you just pretend?"

He looked at the strawberry in his hand, then looked at her, shielding his eyes with his hand and squinting against the sun. She sat on her knees, her Mary Jane shoes and white ruffled socks sticking out from underneath the skirt of her pink jumper. The puffy sleeves of her white blouse were crisp and clean, and her mousy hair was neat beneath the barrettes that held it back. But their rowdy play was evident in her cheeks, which were red from running and from sitting in the sun. She looked like a strawberry herself.

Her lips turned up into a pleasant smile. He felt warm and happy all over. He would give her whatever she wanted.

"I reckon it does look a little like a heart," he said.

"There's my Gabriel," she chirped brightly, her smile widening. She sat a little straighter. The sunlight framed her like a halo from behind. "Now, may I pass?"

"Sure, you can pass."

"You should tell me I can't pass," she whispered, her hand at the side of her mouth. "That might make the story more interesting. Don't you think so?"

He nodded eagerly. "Okay, then. You can't pass."

Abigail placed her hands on her hips and assumed her best pout. "Why not? What's wrong with my heart?"

Gabriel stared at her, waiting for direction.

She brought her hand to the side of her mouth once more.

"Tell me what's wrong with my heart. Go ahead. You can think of it."

She sat smiling, waiting patiently for him. His own heart beat faster as he frantically tried to think of a reason. Desperate, he looked toward the edge of the yard, where Mrs. Wheeler was pulling weeds from her flowerbed, then around the yard and up at the sky. He was struck by a brilliant plot twist, and he held back a grin, proud of himself. He shrugged to appear nonchalant. "There's nothing wrong with it. It's a beautiful heart. It's just that an evil dragon lives in my castle." He held out his hand. "You should keep this somewhere safe." He watched for her reaction, hoping she was impressed.

She smiled and nodded her approval, then turned serious. "Oh, how awful. That won't do at all." She took the strawberry between her fingers. "But what shall I give you as payment?"

A kiss, thought Gabriel, without knowing why. He paused a moment to wonder at the tumbling in his chest.

"It's okay. I don't need any payment," he said.

"You are most kind, sir," said Abigail, bowing her head.

Gabriel watched her as she fussed about, making this plan and that, busily giving instructions to the imaginary people in her world. He felt the odd sensation of wanting to touch her hair. He thought it looked like honey, smooth and soft, as it glistened in the sun. He inhaled deeply, absorbing the thick country summer air. He wasn't sure if it was the air that smelled so sweet, or the strawberries, or her.

It was so quiet here, so much easier to hear one's thoughts than it was at home with all his noisy older brothers. She was so calm, and his time with her was always so peaceful. He listened to her chatter in a dreamlike state, a little awestruck by this power she had, to create such stories in her mind. Her voice was like the melody of a song, with birds twittering and the mellow breeze swishing in the background. He soaked her in like the strawberries soaked in the sunlight.

His eyes were drawn to Mrs. Wheeler, who was watching him as she hunched over, digging a hole with her spade. She waved with her gloved hand and returned her attention to her flowers.

"Look!" cried Abigail, her eyes wide. Gabriel looked. She lowered her hand to a blade of grass. After a moment, she gingerly brought her finger forward.

"A ladybug," said Gabriel, bringing his finger to hers. Their fingertips connected, and he studied them, noticing how small hers was next to his own. The ladybug crawled from her finger to his. Abigail withdrew her hand and sat straight.

"That's good luck," she said. "That's why I gave him to you, you know. Because you're my favorite friend."

Gabriel passed the ladybug from one finger to the next. He leaned forward as he studied it. A crest of blond hair fell over his eyes.

"You could marry me," he said. "You could live with me in my castle forever. That could be your payment."

"Oh, how I wish I could," said Abigail, shaking her head. "But there's a magical spell on me."

"What kind of a spell?"

"I stole a pumpkin from a witch's garden. The witch was hoarding them, and the children in the village were hungry. I sneaked through the gate after midnight and brought one home with me to bake them some bread. She used her crystal ball to find me. According to her spell, I can never marry, but must serve others for as long as I live."

"Oh," he said. He held his fingers straight as the ladybug flew away. "Can't anything break the spell?"

"I must give away my heart, for it was my heart that brought the spell upon me. Oh, prince, don't you see? It's why you simply must take my heart."

Gabriel accepted the strawberry she offered. "Okay," he said. "I'll keep it safe."

"Thataboy, Gabriel," said Mrs. Wheeler. The children turned

to find her stretching into a kneeling position, then spreading her hand on the ground to keep her balance as she stood. She pulled off her gloves and adjusted her hat over her wispy white hair, which was pulled back into a loose, messy bun. She smoothed her gritty hands over the skirt of her striped sundress and joined them in the strawberry patch, squatting beside them with her long dress pushed between her knees. "I knew Lady Abigail could count on you to help her save those children. What a noble prince you are."

"Are you the Queen?" gasped Abigail, her hand at her mouth. She curtsied where she sat. "I am honored, Your Majesty."

"As am I," said Mrs. Wheeler, curtsying in return. "Any lady who is brave enough to defy the witch is a lady I'd like to know." She affected her most serious expression. "You must have been terrified. How did you do it?"

Abigail shrugged. "I thought of the children. They needed me."

"You have done well," said Mrs. Wheeler. She reached downward and plucked a strawberry from the vine. "And because you have broken the spell, you have earned this heart."

Gabriel watched, delighted, as Abigail took the strawberry and kissed it gently. She patted its stem and smiled. "Thank you," she said.

"What a happy ending to this story," Mrs. Wheeler said. Her eyes turned kind as she directed her attention to Gabriel. "Although, I do believe you're both a little young to consider marriage. Best to wait until you're older."

"I don't think I'll get married," said Abigail, shaking her head. "I want to live by myself and tend to my gardens and cook for the soup kitchen, just like you."

"Well, my dear, I was married, a long time ago. You don't remember your grandfather because he died so young. But he was a good man. I was very happy."

"Oh." Abigail thought about this. "Well, maybe I will get married."

"Dear child, you don't have to decide right now," Mrs. Wheeler laughed. "When you grow older, you can do whatever you'd like."

Their conversation was interrupted by the sound of footsteps pounding the grass beside the house. They turned to find an older boy running into the yard, then slowing to a steady stride, swinging his arms as he approached.

"Well, hello there, Patrick," said Mrs. Wheeler. "How are you today?"

Patrick stuck his thumbs under the suspenders that held up his slacks and favored them all with a charming grin. "I'm just swell, Mrs. Wheeler. How are you?"

"Oh, I can't complain. I have my garden, I have the sunshine, and I have these lovely children to keep me company. Are you here to collect your brother?"

"I sure am."

Mrs. Wheeler gestured toward Gabriel. "You heard the man," she told him. "Your mother will be wanting you for dinner. I'm sending Abigail home to her mother, too. You've both probably spoiled your dinners on these strawberries."

Gabriel felt the tug of disappointment as Abigail stood straight and brushed off her dress. "Yes, Mrs. Wheeler," he said as he slowly rose, his knees aching from sitting so long on the ground.

Abigail turned to him and smiled, folding her hands in front of her waist. "Thanks for playing with me, Gabriel. Let's play again tomorrow. You must tell me more about the evil dragon."

"Okay. Unless he eats me first." He pretended to choke himself, opening his eyes wide, sticking out his tongue, and crouching awkwardly over the ground. Patrick chuckled. Mrs. Wheeler laughed.

"Oh, Gabriel," sighed Abigail. "I just don't know what I'm going to do with you."

A wave of joy washed over him as she hugged him, kissed her grandmother, and scampered off down the street toward home.

Patrick, hands in his pockets, began backing up toward the front of the house. Gabriel followed him, turning and waving over his shoulder.

"Bye, Mrs. Wheeler," he said. He smiled politely, his blue eyes gentle. "Thank you for letting me play in your yard again."

"You are most welcome, and thank you for saving the children. Now run along home. I'm sure I'll see you and Abigail tomorrow."

Patrick brought his hand around his brother's back and placed it on his shoulder as they strolled toward the tree-lined sidewalk and started home.

"Hey, buddy. Did you have fun with Abigail today?"

Gabriel nodded and opened his hand to look at the strawberry she had given him.

"What's that for?" asked Patrick.

Gabriel shrugged. "She gave it to me. She was pretending it was her heart."

Patrick grinned. "You sly dog," he said. "How did you get her to give you her heart?"

"It's just a strawberry."

"Sure it is."

Patrick tousled Gabriel's hair and pushed him back playfully, then ran ahead. Gabriel sprang forward and jumped on his back, covering his oldest brother's eyes with his hands. Patrick laughed and threw him off, and the two continued down the street.

"If anyone finds out I'm carrying around this strawberry, I'll be a laughingstock," said Gabriel.

"I won't tell."

They broke into a run, racing each other down the street and into the house, where they joined their parents and brothers at the dinner table. Gabriel held the strawberry in his closed hand, occasionally sneaking a peak at it, happy to have something pleasant to think about as he fell asleep that night.

CHAPTER TWO

DECEMBER, 1966

*G*abriel tilted his head back to observe the high ceilings, then looked around at the long hallways and windows that stretched from the floor to the ceiling, offering a glimpse of the planes awaiting passengers or gliding down the runway before lifting from the ground for the first moments of their journeys. He had never been to the airport before.

Under ordinary circumstances he would have been delighted; he would have liked to take his time, to stand at the window for a while, enjoying the rush of movement and the incredible sounds that vibrated in the floors and shook him in his bones. Today he stared at it blankly, vaguely awed. His gaze returned to his family as they walked ahead of him, holding hands and engaging in quiet conversation. He watched as his mother dabbed at her eyes with a tissue and brought her hand to Patrick's back, resting her head on his shoulder. He acknowledged his own feelings as if from a distance, feeling separated from them by a great gray wall. He knew his mother's gesture affected him, but he was numb.

He turned to Abigail beside him. Her expression was solemn. Her head was straight, her face forward, but her eyes darted here and there at the scene around them, taking in the details as his had.

He sighed and directed his attention once again to his brother Patrick. He barely even recognized him in his crisp green uniform and cap. After two years training as an officer, he seemed a different person. He always had been sharp and confident, but he carried himself with a poise now that he never could have gained in their small Vermont town. Gabriel was both awed and frightened.

Slender fingers slinked through his. He turned to find Abigail watching him. She was so pretty. Momentarily he forgot where he was and what he was doing, and he almost smiled. He cursed himself, ashamed.

The sympathy in her eyes was almost too much to bear, and reality began to seep through the cracks in the wall. His heartbeat quickened, and his eyes widened a little with panic. She squeezed his hand and locked her eyes with his, and he felt better.

The sound of raised voices made him turn his head. Michael, the brother closest to him in age, and his mother were bickering again, but he couldn't tell what about. His father, always the diplomat, was attempting to intervene. Michael's wife Dottie was pushing the carriage, trying to shush her crying baby. Thomas, his second oldest brother, was drifting toward the windows, lured by the planes, and was drawn back brusquely by Michael. Patrick strode forward, straight and tall in his uniform, above it all. Gabriel wished he could see his face.

"I'm so glad I'm here," Abigail whispered, leaning toward him as they walked.

"Me too. Thanks for coming."

"That's what friends are for."

His family stopped at the gate and faced each other, Gabriel and Abigail coming to a halt behind. Gabriel's mother instantly began sobbing.

"No," she cried, wrapping her arms around her oldest son's neck, clutching him. "Please, no. Please don't go. It's going to kill me."

His father rubbed his wife's back as she sniffled. "He's doing the noblest job there is, Harriet. I'm proud of you, son."

Patrick lowered his forehead to his mother's and closed his eyes. "I love you, Mom. I'll be back before you know it."

"God willing," said Michael from behind him.

"You hush, do you hear?" Harriet snapped, separating from Patrick and glaring at him. "If he says he'll be back, he'll be back."

Patrick stepped toward Thomas, who was standing with his hands in his pockets, looking around.

"Hey, brother," Patrick said, clapping him on the back and bringing him in for a tight hug. "I'll see you real soon, okay? Will you help take care of Mom for me?"

Thomas nodded more times than was necessary. He brought his hands from his pockets and put them back in, and shifted his feet a little.

Patrick placed his hands on his shoulders and smiled. "I love you. Do you know that?"

"He doesn't even know what's going on," said Michael.

Gabriel's forehead creased, and anger touched his eyes.

His father lost his diplomacy. "That's enough out of you," said Abe, shaking his finger at Michael. "This isn't the time for your wisecracks."

Harriet put her hands up and closed her eyes. "Please don't be horrible. I can't take it."

"Thomas is smart," inserted Abigail. "He absolutely understands what's happening."

"I won't hear any arguing," said Harriet. "Not now."

"I don't mean any disrespect, Mrs. Kelly. It's just that—"

"Please stop. It isn't helping."

Abigail pursed her lips and was silent.

Patrick said goodbye to Michael and Dottie, kissed the baby, and spent a few moments in upbeat conversation with his father. He hugged his mother for many moments as she cried into his uniform, holding her, occasionally uttering expressions of love and reassurance. Finally he turned to Gabriel, and his face turned solemn.

Gabriel felt blank inside.

"You're leaving me here to deal with them all by myself?" was all he could think of to say.

Patrick suppressed a grin. "You can handle them."

"Not without your help. I may have to kill Michael."

"You'd be doing Dottie a favor."

They both snickered. Gabriel sighed and shoved his hands into his pockets.

"So this is really it," he said. "You're really going."

"It appears that way."

Gabriel shook his head. "How do you stay so strong?"

Patrick indicated his family by tossing his head backward. "I have to be strong for these knuckleheads."

They snickered again.

Gabriel became serious. He felt he shouldn't ask, but he had to. "Are you scared?"

Patrick laughed once, silently, and his smile turned crooked. "Terrified."

Gabriel frowned. A rush of air filled his chest, but he felt as if he couldn't breathe.

"I don't want you to go," he said.

Patrick placed his hands on both his shoulders and looked him in the eye.

"Hey, listen," he told him, his voice quiet so the others couldn't hear. "I told you that between you and me, because we're buddies. It's not like with the others. You'll stay strong for them, won't you? For me?"

Gabriel felt tears forming. He swallowed them back and nodded, then looked to the side, averting his gaze.

"Hey," said Patrick again, to regain his attention.

Gabriel firmed his expression and looked at him. He and Patrick locked eyes.

"I want you to live your life. Don't be afraid to take chances. Buy that house you were thinking about. Live your life."

Patrick's eyes darted toward Abigail, who was watching him.

"Thank you for seeing me off, Abigail," said Patrick, embracing her. He stood back but left his arm around her shoulder. He smiled. "You're like the sister I never had. It means a lot to me that you're here."

"Oh, Patrick, it means a lot to me, too," said Abigail. "I wouldn't be anywhere else right now. I'm honored to be here."

"You finish college, you hear? How much longer do you have, one more year?"

"One more year after this upcoming semester, yes."

"Well, I'll be home in time to see you graduate. So you'd better graduate."

"I will. I promise."

"Keep this one in line for me," said Patrick, wrapping his arm around Gabriel's back and pulling him in close. "He's my favorite."

An announcement called for passengers to board. Patrick lifted his bag from the floor and saluted, then winked at Gabriel. He turned, kissed his mother, waved, and disappeared with even steps onto the plane.

Gabriel felt darkness fill him where he had been empty only moments before. He felt as if invisible weights flowed through his veins, pulling him toward the floor. He stared at his feet, eyes wide, as the sound of his mother's crying reached him from a distance.

He was brought back to the scene before him by the softness of Abigail's hand on his arm. He looked at it without fully registering it. Its lines were firm but gentle, much like Abigail herself. He lifted his gaze to her face, in a haze acknowledging the delicate curves of her figure and the straightness of her posture. Her full pink lips were pulled downward, her eyes fixed on his. They had just been little kids playing house and slaying dragons; Patrick had just been a teenager in suspenders. When did they start fighting wars? How did this happen?

"Are you okay?" she asked.

He nodded absentmindedly. He glanced toward his mother, who was shaking her head and blowing her nose. His father stood beside her, shushing her and rubbing her back.

"I can't believe this is happening," he said.

"Me neither." She shook her head. "He's so brave."

"It makes me feel like I should be with him. Like I should enlist."

"No, God, no!" cried Harriet. Gabriel and Abigail turned to her; she was glaring at him with horror. "No, no, no. Not another one. Not you too. I forbid it. Why would you say such a thing? How could you torment me like this? What is the matter with you?"

Gabriel didn't respond. Abigail tenderly rubbed his back.

"Let's go home," said Michael. "The baby's fussy. There's no point hanging around here."

The family lumbered away from the gate. Gabriel drew Abigail by the arm, holding her back.

"What is it?" she asked kindly, looking up at him.

He stared at her. He wanted to say something, but he didn't know what. She was watching him expectantly. Her eyes were large and upturned, her eyebrows sharp and her cheekbones high —wise, grownup features of the same face he had looked at a thousand times. He blinked and saw her handing him strawberries, running barefoot back and forth between their houses, catching fireflies by the light of the bonfire shooting sparks on the lawn. His chest swelled with the warmth of longing. He wanted to go somewhere with her, to just run away, just live alone blissfully in a simple place where none of this existed. *I love you*, he said in his mind. But aloud he said nothing.

"It's okay," said Abigail, with a soft smile. "I understand. It's a lot to take in."

She took his arm and began walking with him toward his family, who were rather far ahead. He allowed himself a deep breath and tried to relax. He focused on the comfort of being so close to her, the safety in her familiarity.

"Thanks again for coming with me," he said as they meandered around people rushing to meet their flights.

"I couldn't send you without reinforcements," she said, one side of her mouth turning up into a sly grin. "I knew you'd need support."

Their eyes rested on another soldier saying goodbye to his family. Gabriel felt sick, angry, and insignificant, all within seconds. They walked on, leaving their thoughts left unsaid.

"I hope you aren't upset with me for talking back to your mother," Abigail added. "But my heart simply broke for Thomas."

"I'm not upset with you. I think you're an angel."

She smirked. "Rather mouthy angel."

He grinned. "I like my angels mouthy."

She nudged him, and he nudged her back.

"Anyway," she said, "I hope I helped."

"You did. Thank you."

"You are so welcome. It was the least I could do."

They both sighed. Abigail patted his arm.

"I want to spend some time with you today," she said, "to try to take your mind off your troubles. Let's do something silly. Let's see a movie."

"I don't think I want to see a movie. What's the point?"

"Your life will have to go on, Gabriel," she said gently. "Even Patrick said so."

"But everything seems so meaningless."

15

"I know," she said, and patted his arm once more. "You're just going to have to find some meaning in it."

He sighed and wrapped his arm around her shoulder, and she rested her head against his. Together they walked outside and began the long journey home, back to their little town, back to a life that could never be the same again.

CHAPTER THREE

JUNE, 1967

*D*ear Patrick,

I hope you like receiving these letters as much as I like writing them. I really enjoy writing to you. That's why I write so many letters, even when I don't have a lot to say. I like to imagine it's the old days, when we would camp out in the back-yard and fall asleep talking.

I know you want to know how Pop's doing. The short answer is that he's doing as well as you'd expect. He's home now, finally. He goes for physical therapy a few times a week. Mom takes him. It's very hard on both of them. As tough as he is, even Pop can't hide how much pain he's in. I have to be honest. It's hard to see him broken. You know Pop, though. He acts like everything's the same. He says it was just a little fall. He thinks he'll be back to work in no time and that I'm just filling in until then. But we all know he'll never work again. You can't have a bad back if you're a carpenter. I've taken over all his jobs. He sometimes helps me with the books. He's lucky I've been working for him for years and that people trust me. Otherwise I don't know what he would do.

Mom has been hovering over me. She calls me several times a

day and brings over hot dinners. Sometimes she cries and calls me her baby, telling me it would kill her if I were drafted and asking me what they would do. Mom just hasn't been herself. I think it's all too much for her.

Thomas and Michael are the same. Michael is preoccupied with his family and his job. Thomas lives in a world without worries or war, only the faces around him and the flowers in Mom's garden. I think it must be a beautiful world.

But life goes on as normal. I spend my days working, and most of my nights working too. At the end of the day, I'm so tired, I fall asleep as soon as the sun goes down. Sometimes I run errands for Mom and Pop. I don't have a lot of time for friends anymore and even if I did, a lot of them are away at school.

It's hard for me to talk to the family about how worried I am for you. Either their worry makes me more worried, or they're not worried enough, and it makes me angry. I find I'm better off dealing with it alone.

Stay safe. Maybe when you come home we can go camping, just for old times' sake.

Your brother,
Gabriel

THE VILLAGE GREEN was vibrant and cheerful, with streams of sunlight dancing across the grass and through the branches. Gabriel posted his letter and strolled into the center of town, coming to a pause by the maple tree just outside the white fence that enclosed the green. He placed his hands on his hips and squinted against the sunlight at the throngs of merry townspeople reveling in the Founder's Day celebration. The green was a sea of pastel colors, the partygoers having donned their brightest clothes to match the perfect summer day.

Gabriel took in the scene. Quiet cottages lined the streets

surrounding the green, shaded by the birches with their papery pointed leaves. The church with the tall white steeple seemed to overlook the goings on as it sat among the trees on the other end of the green. Beyond the church, in the distance, Gabriel could see the lush mountains of Vermont, seeming to roll on until eternity. He took a deep breath, letting the fresh country air fill his lungs and calm his nerves. Today he would see her again.

His eyes searched the crowd until he spotted her by the gazebo. From this distance, unnoticed, he felt free to watch her before approaching. A smile touched the corners of his eyes. She had a sweet, pretty face, diamond-shaped and strong. Her hair was mousy brown, shoulder-length and flipped upward at the bottom in a dramatic, playful loop. His gaze traveled downward over her long neck and full chest, all made even more beautiful by the straightness of her posture. Gabriel took a moment to admire her coral knit sweater dress. With a pleasant scoop neck and short sleeves, it was suitably modest, but it closely hugged her hourglass form, making it modern and flattering. It was belted at the waist, showcasing the roundness of her hips. He allowed himself to sigh inwardly. She was so much more than he could ever dream of; she was every bit as good-hearted, intelligent, and perfect as she appeared.

Preparing to enter the green, he looked down at his own tall form, slender but strong from his avid hiking and work as a carpenter. Today he had exchanged his usual rugged attire for something more polished. He wore a blue and white striped v-neck pullover and blue trim-cut bellbottom slacks. Though it hadn't been his intention, the blue smoothly complemented his clear blue eyes and golden blond hair, which, perpetually gruff and too long, he had made the effort today to slick back into a thick, more conservative coif. He smoothed down his clothes and hair, sucked in his breath in defiance of the queasiness in the pit of his stomach, and entered the green.

He was sidetracked by his father who, surrounded by his

mother and brothers, was waving to him from the other end of the green. Gabriel reluctantly altered his course and headed in the other direction.

The din of enthusiastic chatter grew louder as he grew closer. His mother, brothers, and sister-in-law appeared unaware of his approach, but his father watched him, a wide grin on his face. Gabriel could hardly hear his father's meek voice as he called to him from the center of the crowd.

"There's my boy," his father said. He was seated, his cane lying next to his chair, while those around him stood. Gabriel squeezed between his mother and Michael, then leaned forward and kissed his father's cheek.

"How are you feeling today, Pop? How's your back?"

Abe rubbed his back. "Oh, it's good, it's good today," he said, nodding, but his smile dimmed, and though it was subtle, Gabriel had the feeling he was hiding a grimace. "I think I'll be back to work in no time."

"Sure you will, Pop," said Gabriel, smiling kindly.

"Where have you been?" asked his mother, finally turning toward him and resting her hand on his back. "I thought maybe you overslept. Is the bachelor life keeping you up too late?"

"Leave the boy alone, Harriet," said Abe, waving his hand in her direction.

"I still don't understand why you bought that big old house," said Harriet. "It's falling apart. It needs all that work. I hate the idea of you living there all by yourself."

"I like fixing it up. And I like the peace and quiet."

"What does a young man in the prime of his life need with peace and quiet?"

"I don't know, Mom," said Gabriel, a little shortly. "It's a good place for thinking. I have a lot to think about."

"Your mother just worries about her baby," said Abe, more tenderly, watching his wife with affection. "Give her some slack." He turned to Gabriel, and his eyes narrowed. "You okay, son?"

Gabriel shrugged. "I'm fine."

Softness touched Harriet's eyes. "You look handsome today. You finally listened to your mother and did something with your hair."

Gabriel brought his hands to the sides of his head and smoothed his hair. "It feels funny."

"Well, it looks great on you."

"How is the house coming?" asked Abe, turning to Gabriel. "Did you get that wall up?"

"Not yet. I have to finish the floor first."

"We've had a letter from Patrick," said Harriet. "It was short this time. He wants you to keep writing him, Gabriel. He specifically told me to tell you that. He says your letters get him through the day."

Gabriel was alarmed by a rush of tears. He forced it back, mortified. "That's good," he mumbled, trying to appear casual.

"Just remember, Gabriel. He's in combat. Keep your letters positive. Write about happy things."

"Yes, ma'am."

"Hey, Gabriel," said Michael, drawing his attention by lifting his drink into the air in his direction. "Next time you write to Patrick, ask him if I can use his truck."

"Unbelievable," said Harriet, shaking her head, her hands on her hips. "How can you be so heartless?"

"What? It's just sitting there."

"You should be ashamed of yourself."

Gabriel turned to Thomas. He patted him on the shoulder. "How are you, my man?"

Thomas shook his head, looking upward. A few moments passed, and he nodded, meeting Gabriel's gaze.

Gabriel was heartened. "Glad to hear it," he said, and smiled.

"Abigail's here," said Abe, motioning with a nod of his chin. "Looks like she's home for the summer."

Gabriel was grateful for this excuse to look in her direction.

She was standing in a cluster of young women. They were a swirl of legs and bold patterns, and with their eager chatter and the enthusiastic movements of their hands, they reminded Gabriel of a flock of pretty, colorful birds.

"I'm surprised she came back here," Harriet said snidely. "I was sure this town would be too small for her. That girl and her bright ideas. I think she's grown too big for her britches."

"Abigail's always been outspoken, Mom," said Gabriel. "That isn't anything new."

"She seems rather more so since school."

"I don't think so."

But Harriet had been distracted by Michael's crying baby; she was taking her from Dottie's arms. She and Michael bickered over the best way to quiet her.

"Don't you want to go on over and say hello to Abigail?" asked Abe. "You haven't seen her since winter."

Gabriel shrugged, not wanting to appear too obvious. "Yeah, sure. Sure, I'll go say hello."

He cleared his throat, squared his shoulders, and prepared to walk away. Abe called him back.

"Just one thing, son."

Gabriel stopped and turned toward his father. Abe motioned toward him with his finger, and Gabriel bent downward.

"Maybe it's time to tell her," Abe said.

Gabriel blanched. "What do you mean?"

"What do you mean, what do I mean? I may be nearly crippled, but I'm not blind."

Gabriel sighed and straightened. "I don't know. I'll see."

"Life's too short, son. What are you waiting for?"

Gabriel sighed again and watched Abigail for a moment before responding. A group of well-groomed young men had joined the women, smiling and joking, showing off for each other now that they were home from college. Abigail was in the center of the crowd, laughing now, her head held high.

"Don't be intimidated," said Abe, seeming to read his thoughts. "You're every bit as good as they are."

"They don't intimidate me. I don't give a damn about them."

"What's the problem, then?"

"Oh, I don't know," said Gabriel, shoving his hands into his pockets and looking at the ground. "I'm not her type."

"You're being foolish, son," said Abe, but his face was kind. "You're enough her type to have been her friend for all these years."

"She's just a friend."

"Does she know you're sweet on her?"

"No. I don't think so."

"Well, I suggest you change that. Go on."

Gabriel patted his father on the back and let him squeeze his hand, then affected an air of confidence and sauntered off.

At his approach, a few of the women noticed him. "Hi, Gabriel," they said, smiling sweetly, and waving demurely with their fingers.

"Hi."

Abigail turned her head. Instantly her face brightened, and she touched the shoulder of the woman to whom she had been speaking, asking her to give her a moment.

"Hey there, Gabriel!" she greeted him, taking his hands in hers and kissing his cheeks. He indulged in a deep breath, savoring her floral scent. He shivered as the skin of her cheek brushed his, and he was disappointed when she pulled away. "I was hoping you'd be here! Gosh, I've missed you."

At the sound of her voice, the voice he knew so well, his reservations dissipated. She was warm, vibrant, and at ease with him—she was exactly the same. He could only be excited to see her. He was unable to keep himself from smiling, and his eyes crinkled in the corners. "I'm here to see you, Abby. I wouldn't miss a chance to see my favorite girl."

"Am I really your favorite?" she teased. She tilted her head, a little coyly. "You mean there's no foxy girl in your life?"

"As far as I'm concerned, you're the only girl in the world," he said, encouraged by her flirtatiousness. "You're one of a kind. Maybe there are other girls, but I only have eyes for you."

"Are you going to start singing now?"

"I just might."

"Stop flattering me." She playfully slapped his arm. "You're making me blush."

"You look cute when you blush," he told her, his voice growing mischievous. He pinched her face. "Like you have strawberries on your cheeks."

"Now you really are flattering me," she groaned, but her eyes sparkled.

Gabriel went on, delighted by her responses. "It reminds me of the time we ate all the strawberries in your grandmother's strawberry patch. Your cheeks were stained pink for days."

"My mother made me skip dessert for a week after that," Abigail said. She shook her head, feigning regret. "I should have known better than to listen to you, Gabriel Kelly. You were always getting me into trouble."

A stray crest of hair fell over his eyes, and he brushed it away. He watched her as she scanned the party. Her warmth was evident in her eyes, which were brown like his morning coffee, and in the long, upward sweep of her lashes. He liked how she was wearing her hair now, with her bangs curved to the side. But what really drew him were her lips. They were full and painted pink, a pink that reminded him of strawberry candy. He wondered if they tasted as sweet as they looked, and resisted the urge to lick his own lips.

"Gabriel," sounded another voice, drawing him from his reveries. One of the young women approached, placed her hand on Abigail's shoulder, and shifted her weight to one hip. Rosie Cutler's hair was a short dark bob, crowned neatly on top with a large white bow. Her short striped dress, A-lined and brightly colored, showed off her legs, as did her tall wedge shoes. Rosie worked full time as a teller at the bank where Abigail worked on her vacations from school; the three of them had graduated high school together, but Rosie and Abigail had only grown close in recent years. "How's your house coming along?" she asked him with a smile.

"It's coming along great, Rosie. It's really something. It's got missing floors and rotting wood, and it's old as hell, but it's good and sturdy, and I love it."

"Is it right in town?"

"It's only a few blocks from my folks' house, yeah."

"I still think it's amazing that you bought a house," interjected Abigail. "What an accomplishment, Gabriel. How did you do it?"

"I've been saving money ever since I started working for my dad, and I've been working almost around the clock now that he's hurt his back. I got the house pretty cheap because it needs so much work. I'm fixing it up myself."

"Your dad put so much of himself into his work. I'm sure it's killing him to have to stop."

"It's not easy for him, but with me helping out, at least the work's staying in the family."

"It's wonderful that you're taking care of your family and using your talents to make a life for yourself. I'm so proud of you." She smiled warmly, and he swelled with pride.

"Thanks, Abby. That means a lot to me. Especially coming from you," he added, wishing ruefully that he could stop grinning. "I can't believe you're getting ready to start your last year of college. Now, that's something to be proud of. I know I couldn't do it."

"Oh, sure you could," she said, tapping his arm. "You can do anything you put your mind to."

The three chatted for a couple of minutes, throngs of people mingling and dancing on the lawn.

"Has there been any news of your brother, Rosie?" asked Gabriel.

"We get letters. He tries to remain upbeat. We just cherish every word and don't watch the news."

"Well, we're praying for you. For you, for your folks, and of course for Danny. We know how hard it is."

"Thanks, Gabriel. We're praying for Patrick, too. How are you holding up?"

"The best I can," said Gabriel, his voice growing dark. "But I hate it. I just wish he were home."

"I can't imagine how hard this must be for you," said Abigail, frowning. She laid her hand on his arm. "I haven't stopped worrying for a minute since he left. I think of Patrick every day. He's like my brother, too."

"He sure is, Abby. Thanks."

"Did I tell you I participated in sit-ins against the war when I was at school?" asked Abigail. "It was one of the most powerful experiences of my life. It made me feel that I was part of something, that I could make a difference."

"It's swell that you're helping to bring change. I just wish it were easier. It's hard not to let it get you down."

"If it's important enough, you do it anyway. Nothing worth doing is easy."

"But change takes so long, and my brother's over there now. They could send me too. I mean, nothing's stopping them from sending me, too."

His voice had begun rising. Several people turned to look at him. He swallowed and calmed himself.

"I just don't know how not to be mad about it," he grumbled.

"I think you have every right to be mad," she said gently. "But try not to be cynical. We can't accomplish anything by doing nothing. If we believe in something, we should fight for it, and I want to bring Patrick home."

"I really want to believe that, Abby. I want to bring him home, too."

One of the men nearby overheard their conversation. "I don't blame you," he said, his hands in his pockets as he rocked casually back and forth from his heels to his toes. "He's got no business being over there in the first place."

Gabriel and Abigail turned their heads in his direction. Gabriel felt fury consume him like fire.

"Mind your own damn business," he seethed.

"It's my business when my country practices imperialism under the guise of freedom. It's my business when my neighbors condone it."

"Really, now, Walter," said Abigail. "You know the Kellys better than that. Now's not the time for you to stand on your soapbox."

"I don't know what you're so upset about, Abigail. You no more support this war than I do."

"But I support my friends who are caught in the middle. This war is not their fault."

"Like hell it isn't."

Gabriel stepped forward in spite of himself. His heart was pounding so fast it was blurring his vision. "You're talking about my brother," he said, making himself calm. His voice, though flat and quiet, was tense. "You're talking about Rosie's."

"Yeah, watch it," said Rosie. "They're heroes who answered their country when called. They're off fighting so you can go to school. You should be thanking them."

"How about you ladies go gossip somewhere else and let us work out the heavy issues ourselves."

Abigail grimaced. "We're perfectly capable of carrying on an intelligent conversation. We have brains, you know."

"Oh, is that what you call them, dear?"

The men in the group laughed.

"You're a piece of work, Walter," said Abigail as the snickering subsided. "You think you're showing off, but you only look ignorant when you tell such jokes. It's ironic."

"That's a mighty big word there."

"Shall I explain it to you?"

"Look out, boys," called the man beside Walter, holding out his hands, a cocky grin on his face. "We've stumbled across a modern woman. I hope she doesn't eat us alive."

"Doug, Abigail is an educated woman," Gabriel called back. "What the hell could she possibly want with you?"

Everyone laughed again. Doug guzzled the drink in his hand and glared at them.

"We all used to hang out, Gabriel," he said, shaking his head. "You used to be fun. You sure have changed." He and his friends strode off.

Gabriel returned his attention to Abigail. "Not all of us are jackasses."

She smiled. "You don't have to convince me of that."

They talked for a minute or two about what had happened but didn't want to linger on the unpleasantness. The conversation lightened. Abigail asked him about his work.

"Work is great," said Gabriel. "Building a house from the ground up, knowing I made it with my own two hands, there just isn't anything like it."

"It's beautiful to hear you talk like that. See, you can make change happen if you only work hard enough. You can create big things and make a difference. "

Gabriel smiled, and his heart warmed. "Maybe you're right."

"And now," a voice boomed from the gazebo behind them—Gabriel turned to see the mayor standing with a bullhorn to his lips—"the Women's Club would like to remind you of the annual pie baking contest to be held on the 4th of July! The winner will receive a trophy and a dinner for two at Jane's Restaurant. We hope you all will consider entering. Also this year, we will be collecting baked goods to send to our brave boys overseas. Thank you, and enjoy the day!"

Applause and lively chatter sounded, and Abigail's friends dissipated into the crowd. Abigail and Gabriel clapped, as well, then turned to each other when the mayor had left the gazebo.

Abigail smiled. "I think I'll enter that contest," she said. "I want to help the soldiers. And I want to be part of this town again."

"Great idea. No one can bake like you can."

"I'll have to come up with something really special. And if I do win, I insist that you come to Jane's with me. It's been so long since we've had one of our long chats. Won't that be a gas?"

"It sure will," he told her, his blue eyes crinkling at the corners.

"Now, the big question: what kind of pie?" She brought her thumb and index finger to her chin and frowned. "What do you think, Gabriel? What kind of pie makes you happy?"

"Strawberry, of course. Is there any other kind?"

"Well, there you have it. Strawberry it is. You'll have to be my taste tester to let me know if I'm on the right track."

Something happened inside him at these words, and he watched her earnestly as his future with her flashed before his eyes. He could perfectly envision it, tasting her strawberry pie after happy family dinners, the house they would fix together, their cozy days and glorious nights. He saw her as a mother and as a grandmother; he imagined the quiet of their mornings as they sat together decades later, reminiscing about the life they had shared.

He saw it as clearly as he saw her face in the sunlight, and suddenly he felt sure of himself and free.

"Sure, I'll help you," he began, not believing what he was about to say but prepared to say it anyway, curious to see where it would lead. *What the hell have I got to lose?* he asked himself. "But the deal is, if you win, you have to do something for me."

"What's that?"

"Marry me."

Her eyes grew round. "What are you talking about?"

"I'm talking about the fact that I love you," he said. "I'm sorry, but I do. I really do."

Abigail watched him for a moment, stunned silent. Then she laughed and slapped his arm. "Oh, what a hoot you are! You almost had me for a minute there. You don't want to marry me."

"Sure I do."

She looked at him slyly, her face bright. "But only if I can bake a good pie?" she joked. "Come on, it's 1967. I'm working toward a degree."

"I know. It makes me want to marry you even more."

She frowned now, her eyes growing serious. "You're kidding with me—right?"

He shook his head. "No. I'm not kidding. And it's not just because you can bake a good pie. You've known me all your life, Abby. How could you not know that?"

Her frown deepened. He couldn't read her expression.

"Oh hell, I'm sorry," he sputtered, panicking that he had offended her. "I don't care about your pie. I mean, I do care about your pie. I love your pie. Your pie is delicious. The best, in fact." He was sweating now, and he could feel his face turning red. *Stop talking*, he scolded himself, horrified. "But that's not all I care about. Obviously. I didn't mean I only want you as a wife if you can bake a good pie. The pie has nothing to do with it. I meant what I said about my feelings. I love you." *You're still talking. Why are you still talking?* He desperately wanted to rub his sweaty hands on his pants, but he restrained himself. He swallowed. "Please don't be upset about the pie. I said it on an impulse because I thought it was a good way to finally tell you how I feel. I was trying to be funny, but I wasn't funny. I was serious. I want to marry you. I'm serious." *Oh, my God*, he thought, closing his eyes.

She didn't say anything in response. Fortifying himself, he

opened his eyes. Her nose and eyes were red. He could tell she was attempting to hold back tears.

"How long have you felt this way?" she managed to utter after a few moments had passed.

She wasn't yelling at him or laughing. He recovered somewhat, though his heart was pounding. "Always. Ever since we were kids."

She closed her eyes and lowered her head, and clasped her hands together in front of her face.

He took the handkerchief out of his pocket and handed it to her.

She dabbed at her eyes, sniffled, and looked up at him, more composed.

"Why didn't you say anything?"

His brows drew together, and a corner of his mouth lifted. "I was worried I'd start babbling incoherently."

She laughed and covered her mouth, then dabbed her eyes again.

He shrugged, turning solemn. "We were just friends. You seemed so high above me, and you had such smart boyfriends. I was just some guy from down the street who followed you around like a puppy. I guess I felt like I didn't have a chance, that I didn't measure up."

"Oh, Gabriel. My sweet friend. Did I ever make you feel that way?"

"Abby, you're the nicest person in the world. I've never felt anything but happy with you. You make me feel better than anybody. That's the whole point."

Her face crinkled. He brought his fingers to her cheek and wiped a tear that was sliding toward her chin, then fiddled with the hair around her ear.

"Should we give it a go, Abby?" he asked softly. His heart was pounding, and he was rapidly losing confidence as she put off answering his question.

The tension of the conversation was interrupted by the mayor, who once again took to the gazebo, this time to announce the arrival of the bluegrass band. The musicians began playing a lively, upbeat tune. Gabriel and Abigail watched them mindlessly, gathering their thoughts.

She looked at him squarely. "This is happening very fast. I have to think about all this."

"I understand," he said, disappointed, but also relieved she had not rejected him right away.

She studied him for a few moments. "Let's spend some time together, okay? Then we'll see."

"Okay." He suppressed a sigh. Of course she wouldn't say yes. He was stupid to have asked her. Though he didn't blame her, he felt his heart splitting apart as longing and embarrassment replaced his boneheaded excitement. And he was furious with himself for putting this strain on their friendship; he feared they would never be able to recapture their easy intimacy.

The pity in her expression made it worse, and he wished he could disappear. But then, eyes locked with his, she took his hand. He took a few deep breaths as warm waves coursed through his blood. When she squeezed his hand and clasped it tight for the duration of the concert, he could only feel hopeful and alive.

EVERY TIME THE DOOR OPENED, Abigail's heart flipped. This last time, she had almost dropped her ladle into her pot of soup. *Damn it,* she scolded herself, closing her eyes a moment to regain her composure. *It's only Gabriel. Calm the hell down.*

She was nervous but excited. She hadn't seen him since Founder's Day, when he had told her he loved her and asked her to marry him if she won the pie contest. That was a week ago; for days, each was too bashful to call the other. Meanwhile, she had done nothing but agonize over it every moment since. Finally she had called him, figuring he wouldn't be brave enough to do it himself and that he was probably being a gentleman by leaving the next move to her.

"Earth to Abigail," sounded a voice beside her. Abigail turned to find that Rosie had joined her behind the table at the head of the room, tying her apron behind her back.

"Sorry, Rosie. What were you saying?"

"I was asking if you were sure he was coming."

"I have no reason to think that he won't," said Abigail, her heart flipping again as the door opened. She jerked her head upward, only to see another kind face in search of a warm meal. She smiled sincerely as he approached the table, scooped some soup into his bowl, and nodded in welcome as he offered his humble thanks and walked away.

Abigail frowned and turned the soup over a few times with her ladle.

From beside her, Rosie spoke again.

"Can I ask you something?"

Abigail looked at her.

"Why didn't you tell him you love him too?"

Abigail's frown deepened, and she returned her attention to her soup.

"I don't know," she said with a sigh. "I was tempted to say yes, but it was happening so fast. It was such a surprise. I was flustered."

Rosie scrunched up her face, showing her skepticism. "You don't mean to tell me you never knew he had feelings for you."

"I suspected he might," Abigail said before pausing to serve a couple of people who had approached the table. "But he never said anything about it, so I figured it was only wishful thinking. He was so grounded and serious. I thought I was too dreamy for him, always with my head in the clouds."

"Well, you never said anything to him, either."

"I guess not."

"So why not tell him now?"

They served bowls of soup to a young family of four and watched them sit at a table to the side.

Abigail turned to Rosie once more.

"I don't want to damage our friendship," she said. "It means so much to me. If we try to make it more and it doesn't work out, what will happen to us then? Would we ever be able to go back?"

"I understand, Abby. I'd just hate for fear to keep you two apart."

"But what if we ruin it?"

"Well, what if you don't?"

Abigail frowned and straightened some silverware on the table. "It's not just that. I'm not opposed to getting married one day, but I also want to accomplish something with my life. Too many men in this town just aren't on board. I could never be in a marriage that wasn't equal."

"I understand. But this is Gabriel."

"Yes, it is." She paused a moment. "I'm going to be honest, Rosie. I love Gabriel, sure. But I also think we see the world differently, and I don't know that we'd be a good fit. I want someone with an open mind, not only about men and women but also about life. I want him to see possibilities, to enjoy things, to take advantage of experiences—not be burdened by doubt. And it wouldn't be fair to either of us if I'm not completely sure." She furrowed her brow. "Does that make sense?"

"Yes," Rosie said. "It makes perfect sense."

Abigail sucked in her breath as the door opened. A woman walked in. Abigail relaxed her shoulders and smoothed back her hair.

"Anyway, it's all so sudden. I can't make this kind of decision lightly. I'm still in school, for heaven's sake. I figure spending time together first won't hurt. This way we'll know for sure that it's right."

The door opened again. This time, Abigail's anticipation was rewarded. In stepped Gabriel, dressed more casually today in a plain white shirt, tucked neatly into his jeans. His hair was more natural, as well, its too-long crests hanging over the sides of his face and the back of his neck. Abigail's chest filled with tenderness. This was much better. Though he had looked debonair and stylish on Founder's Day, that fancy appearance simply wasn't Gabriel. At the sight of him today—his tall, strong frame, thick shoulders and arms rounded with tight, perfect muscles—she felt her breath quicken and her palms sweat. She rubbed her hands nervously over the front of her crisp pink dress.

He spotted them behind the table and smiled. Abigail felt her heart melt. As he approached, all her past attraction to him flooded her in a rush. He had been her best friend for years. But he had also been a handsome, delightfully rough distraction from the seriousness of her own life. Countless times she had eyed him as they fished together in the creek behind his parents' house or hung her mother's laundry on the clothesline, admiring the rugged, angular features of his face, his sharp nose and square jaw. She loved the physical nature of his work; she loved watching the way his arms and hands moved as he put up walls or built furniture from scraps. But what really drew her were his eyes. Deep and earnest, they were as blue as the sky under which they had played, and they crinkled kindly in the corners when he smiled. She had never seen eyes so pure. To her they represented his honesty and clarity: he was realistic and level-headed, the perfect complement to her idealism.

"You made it," she announced a little too cheerily as he reached for the apron handed to him by Rosie. "I was beginning to worry."

He looked at his watch. "I'm right on time."

She glanced at her own watch but didn't see it. "Oh. So you are."

He walked behind the table and stood beside her.

"Gabriel, you take my ladle," said Rosie. "I'm going to prepare some more potatoes."

Abigail watched Rosie as she disappeared into the back room, then swallowed and looked at Gabriel, whose eyes were on her. She calmed somewhat. *It's only Gabriel*, she told herself again. She smiled, relieved.

"Thanks for coming," she said. "I know it's a bit of a drive to the city."

"It was no problem. I like going for drives."

"I thought this was the perfect way to start our time together."

"It is," he agreed. "It's something that's important to you."

"Important to everyone," she corrected, and swept her arm forward, indicating the people sitting at the tables before them.

An elderly couple approached the table. Abigail smiled and nudged Gabriel's arm with her elbow.

Gabriel sprang to life. "How are you, my friends?" he asked as he scooped soup into two bowls, then took them in his own strong hands. "Where would you like to sit today?"

Abigail watched him walk away, the couple hobbling behind. She allowed herself to sigh aloud.

A rush of people entered. Gabriel and Abigail greeted and served them, then stood looking around, satisfied.

"This is good," he said quietly, nodding. He turned to her. "How often do you come here?"

"When I'm off from school, I come here once a week. I'd like to come more often, but it's hard to juggle with work."

"Are you going to work at the bank again?"

"Yes, and I'm determined to earn a promotion after I graduate. There are so few women in managerial positions." She threw him a crooked smile. "I like the idea of shaking things up in our little town."

"Me too. Give 'em hell."

"I'm going to try. For now, though, the hours are good, which means I'll have the chance to look into business school. I'd love to go into government someday. While I'm here, I'm going to start a women's study group, just a weekly discussion to talk about things that matter. I don't want to slow down just because I'm home from school."

"See, there's lots you can do in Linsbury," said Gabriel. He smiled at her. "My mother said she was surprised you wanted to come back."

"I'm sure she did," Abigail muttered with a smirk.

"Why is that?"

Abigail fussed with the tablecloth, smoothing its wrinkles, hesitating as she debated what to say. "I saw her on Founder's Day, before you arrived," she said after a couple of seconds had passed. "I told her about some of my plans. She didn't seem impressed." She paused again. "I don't think she's so taken with me anymore."

"Sure she is. She's just edgy lately."

"Yes. You're probably right."

Rosie hustled out from the kitchen and squeezed between them, dumping more soup into their pots. She scuffled away, leaving them alone once more.

"How about you?" Abigail asked him. "Did you ever think about leaving town?"

"No. My roots are in Linsbury. My job is in Linsbury. I have stability in Linsbury. The rest of the world is a messed up place. I've got no need for it."

"That's rather morbid," said Abigail, raising her eyebrows as she served a young woman and replaced her ladle in her pot. "I don't like to look at things that way."

"I don't either, but that's reality."

Abigail faced him. "I know you're worried about Patrick. It's okay to be afraid."

Gabriel was spooning soup into a man's bowl. He smiled awkwardly but said nothing.

After serving a few more people he placed both hands on the table, leaned forward, and sighed. "Unfortunately even our little town's not the same anymore. There are yellow ribbons every-where. You walk up Main Street, and you ask people if they've heard from their brothers or husbands or sons."

"People are coming together in a crisis and caring for each other. It's made the community even stronger. I think that shows that there's goodness everywhere."

"I don't know how you do it."

"How I do what?"

"How you keep such a positive attitude with everything going on in the world."

"You mean how we can send people into space? How we're making advancements in civil rights every day?"

Gabriel filled a bowl for a thin young woman in tattered clothing who avoided his gaze, then for a couple with a little child. "So much happens that's beyond our control. It makes a person feel so small."

Abigail faced him. "That's why I do this. I'm just one person, but I can be a cog in the wheel. If I affect one life, what will that person do for someone else in return?"

He shook his head as he cleaned up some spilled soup with a towel. "You're amazing, Abby. You always see the good in things. I wish I had your confidence."

"You've got plenty of confidence. Just look at you, with a house and a business. You had the confidence to go after those things. You even had the confidence to ask me to marry you." She blushed and giggled, then brought herself under control. "You don't give yourself enough credit."

"That isn't confidence," he said, shaking his head once more. "It's just that I'm older now, and I see how things work. I mean, I could be drafted tomorrow and then I won't have the chance."

"I think you should cross that bridge when you come to it."

He slowed the circular motion of his hand as it cleaned the table, but he remained silent.

She watched him curiously. His jaw was tight, his eyes intent.

"What's the matter?" she asked.

"Nothing," he said. "It's nothing."

Before she could encourage him to say more, a little boy approached the table and eyed the bread bowl, then looked between Gabriel and Abigail. Gabriel held the bowl closer for him. The boy picked a hunk of bread from the bowl and scampered away.

"That's a pretty neat feeling," said Gabriel. "I'll give you that."

Their eyes met, and her heart skipped a couple of beats. He smiled, and she felt a little dizzy.

"That's great," she uttered, her face flushing. She turned back to her soup.

They stood for a few moments in silence. Finally, she smiled.

"You're just like you were when we were kids, you know? Pensive and honest, and maybe a little cynical. But I think deep down you're just as idealistic as I am."

"That's just your idealism talking."

She chuckled and nudged him with her elbow. "I'm serious. You always meet me halfway."

"You're exactly the same, too. A ray of sunshine. Always assuming the best."

They worked together, helping dozens of people and chatting about their lives and hopes for the future. They shared stories and laughter, and by the end of the day, they felt like it was old times. They hung up their aprons tired and smelling of soup, but happy.

Outside, he walked her to her car, a pale yellow Volkswagon. They faced each other before going their separate ways and driving home.

"I'm glad we did this," he said. "I feel like I made a little difference today." He smiled. "Thank you."

Her blood tingled; she felt giddy and excited. "You're welcome."

She didn't know what to do next. Her gaze darted here and there, avoiding his.

"Well," he said. "I guess I'll see you soon."

Her throat was dry, and she swallowed. "I guess so."

His eyes were serious, and he opened his mouth as if he would say something, but he didn't. He leaned toward her for a moment, then checked himself, and stood straight. Finally, he steadied his jaw and leaned toward her once more. Abigail caught a glimpse of his closing eyes as instinctively she closed her own eyes and raised her chin. He kissed her cheek, softly, letting his lips linger for an extra moment or two before pulling away. He stood straight again, but closer; she could see his rushed breathing in the rising and falling of his chest, but the sound was drowned out by the sound of her own.

"Bye, Abby," he said, and opened her door.

"Bye," she whispered in return. He closed the door gently after her, smiled and waved, and backed up a few paces for her to pull out of her spot and drive away.

"BAKING A PIE, LOVE?"

Abigail's eyes scanned the ingredients spread in a neat line along the white linoleum kitchen countertop. She nodded solemnly.

"Yes, I think so," she told her older sister.

They stood still, in silence. Marion raised her eyebrows and popped her bubblegum.

"Something wrong, love?"

Abigail smiled and directed her attention to the countertop. "No, no. Nothing's wrong." She opened the canister that contained the flour and began scooping it into a large ceramic bowl. "Do you have a date with Jack tonight?" Jack was Marion's fiancé. They were getting married in the fall.

Marion stared at her, then glanced down at her pink pajamas, floral robe, and fuzzy white slippers. "It's Wednesday. I just finished grading papers."

"Of course. That makes sense, of course."

"You sure you're all right?"

"Of course. I was just thinking."

"Oh," Marion said. She popped her bubblegum again. "You're acting funny."

"Am I?" Abigail asked, looking at her sister, her smile brightening. "I'm sorry, Marion." She turned back to the counter and dug into the sugar with her scoop. "I was just wondering if I ought to add some brown sugar to this pie. It would be risky, I know! I can't believe I'm even suggesting it." She paused, closed her eyes, and shook her head, attempting to clear it. "I'm really overthinking this."

"It's just a pie."

Abigail nodded, biting her lower lip. Marion eyed her curiously as she slid a magazine off the white formica table and exited the room. *Just a pie*, Abigail said to herself. *If only*.

She set to work, adding from memory the ingredients for her strawberry pie. She had made this pie a thousand times and wasn't even sure why she felt compelled to practice; she knew this pie was fabulous. She had watched her grandmother perfect the recipe, had spent years learning about the balance and the chemistry of baking. Her grandmother had sent her to collect the strawberries herself and treated her as an apprentice who had earned possession of the secrets of the pie.

She cut in the butter and formed the dough into a neat ball. As she rolled it out and shaped it into crust, she thought of his face when he told her he loved her, and a warm rush made her face flush, then seeped downward through her chest, core, and all the way through her legs to her feet, weakening her knees. She began cutting the strawberries and thought of how they used to sit in her grandmother's strawberry patch; she remembered how she had pretended a strawberry was her heart and made him take it. Now look at them, all grown up and headed toward a conclusion they possibly had anticipated all along.

She pressed the crust into the dish. The pie was beginning to take shape. As she dumped the strawberry mixture into the crust, she was pleased by its appearance. She loved that coming home had given her an opportunity to spend time with him again, and she was grateful that they remained comfortable together. She liked that he had so willingly met her at the soup kitchen and that he had appreciated the importance of their work there; she had enjoyed their conversation, even if they disagreed at times.

She pinched the sides of the crust together and shoved the pie into the oven. She had to chuckle a little at the idea that she was baking a pie for a man. She had spent so much of her time in college thinking about and discussing how there was so much more for women. She thought of how Gabriel had helped her defend herself on Founder's Day and how he had always respected her opinions—and she was glad he understood that the pie wasn't symbolic of the kind of wife she'd be. In fact, she felt that most men wouldn't understand her baking this pie: the progressive men she knew at school wouldn't hear of it, and the more traditional men in town wouldn't see the humor in it. With Gabriel, it was easy and free, the perfect balance. She liked that she could bake him a pie without his making assumptions about the role she'd take in the future.

She stood back for a moment, thinking—she felt it needed something more, a special ingredient, but for now she decided to rely on the original recipe that had worked for years. She set the timer and sat back to wait, eager for the sweet aroma of pie to fill her kitchen. She was prepared to go along with this adventure and see where it led. Maybe she was thinking too hard. A man she loved had proposed to her, had confessed he had loved her as long as she loved him. She smiled, put these thoughts out of her mind, and focused on her pie. She would have to put everything into it.

She would have to make sure it was the best pie she had ever made.

Dear Patrick,

Mom says I should only write about happy things in my letters to you. I'll start by thanking you for sending us the pictures. We look at them over and over. It feels strange to see you in a combat uniform, but it makes me proud, too. We read your descriptions of the men and the landscape with fascination. Though I've noticed you don't tell us much about what goes on there. I imagine you don't want to worry us.

Happy things. My house is coming along. It's still barely anything more than a pile of scrap wood, but I'm fixing it little by little. It's a big house, much bigger than what I need. I don't even know why I bought the damn thing. Maybe it was the porch. That porch called to me. You can help me fix it up when you come home, unless I'm over there too by then.

Mom says she won't let her baby fight in a war while her oldest is there, too. She's convinced I won't be drafted, that with Pop not working I'm the breadwinner now and that I can get a defer-ment. I myself have mixed feelings. I don't really believe in the war, and I want to live my life and fix up my house. I like running Dad's business. But I hate that you're there and I'm not. I don't want to go, but I don't want to not go, either. It's kind of funny when you think about it.

I can see Mom unraveling. There's nothing specific that makes me say that. It's one thing here, another there. She frets all the time. She's short-tempered. She can't stay focused on anything. She's spending so much time helping Pop that she doesn't have any patience left for Thomas, who needs it most. So I try to pick up the slack.

I guess I wasn't supposed to talk about that. Everything else seems so meaningless, though. I fixed my truck, should I tell you about that? Somehow I don't think it's that important. It's hard for me to care about much of anything these days.

I read to Thomas a lot. We walk around the neighborhood together. I know Mom has extra responsibilities taking care of him and that she worries about what will happen to him when she and Pop are gone. But the time I spend with him is always peaceful and happy, and free of care. I think he's with us for a reason. I know that's sappy, but it's the truth. He gives me hope. I can't explain it, so I won't even try.

I hope it isn't too rough where you are, but I know it is. I see it on the news every night. The images scare me, but I look at them anyway. If you have to live it, the least I can do is watch it.

Happy things. I went to the Founder's Day celebration. I wasn't going to go, but I wanted to see Abigail again. I'm going to tell you something funny, are you ready? I asked Abigail to marry me. I know, crazy. I'll bet you didn't see that coming. Would it surprise you if I told you I've always been in love with her? Did you know? Pop says he knew. I wonder if she knew, too. I wonder if everyone knew. You're probably wondering why I asked her to marry me out of the blue like that. I'm kind of wondering that myself. It seemed right at the time, but now I wish I could take it back. It's not that I don't want to marry her. But asking someone to marry you tends to change things between you. Especially if she says she has to think about it.

I wouldn't mind if you wrote me separately from the others. You wouldn't have to protect me. But I know you've got more to do than sit around writing letters all day. So I won't sweat it.

You were always the one to pay attention to me and include me. Being the oldest, you could have brushed me off, but you didn't. I appreciate that. Have I ever told you that before? I just thought you should know.

I don't understand how I can be both a baby and a breadwinner. Those two things seem to contradict each other, but that's mothers for you.

Stay safe.

Your brother,

Gabriel

~

"I LIKE BEING BACK HERE with you," Abigail said, trying to act casually even as her heart fluttered with excitement and anticipation. "It feels just like old times."

They were walking up the steps toward her grandmother's front door. When she had arrived, she had found him sitting waiting for her on the steps of the porch. Abigail and her mother were visiting with Mrs. Wheeler that afternoon, and Abigail had invited Gabriel along to keep her company and help her pick strawberries for her pie. She was looking forward to seeing her mother and grandmother, but she felt giddy at the idea of spending time alone with Gabriel after.

"Maybe you can tell me one of your stories," he said, turning to her as they reached the top step, a kind smile crossing his lips and his eyes crinkling in the corners.

They crossed the porch, the floorboards creaking under their feet. "Me and my stories," she muttered, tucking her hair behind her ear, embarrassed. "I was such a dreamy, flaky kid." She laughed a little in spite of herself.

"You had hungry children to save. It was very important." His smile turned tight-lipped; she could tell he was trying to keep it from widening. "You had the morals of a saint, even back then. You were like no other kid. It was something else."

"I was something else, all right."

They paused by the front door and faced each other. His

expression turned more serious. "I don't think you know how much it meant to me," he said. "I used to love listening to your stories. I never knew where we'd be going, but I always knew there would be magic." He stuck his hands in his pockets, looking at her frankly. "I lived for those times."

Warmth filled her, and she grew a little dizzy at the sincerity of these words. "That's wonderful," she said, her voice a near whisper. "I had no idea the stories had such an effect on you. They were so silly."

"Not to me. I have three older brothers. I guess it was easy to feel lost. The stories were something just for me. Well, for us." He locked eyes with her. "I took them very seriously."

"I'm glad," she said airily, feeling light-headed. She turned crimson, amazed by her bashfulness. She could see her own chest rising and falling, and willed her breathing to slow.

"If you really want to make it like old times," he said, grinning, "you'll have to call me a prince and chase me through the clotheslines."

She summoned her bravery and looked at his face. He was watching her intently, his blue eyes sharply focused, his square jaw set. He was wearing a cheerful blue and white plaid shirt with a crisp, tidy collar. It was tucked neatly into light-colored flat front jeans. He stood with his arms at his sides, and Abigail could tell he had been working outside in the sun; his skin was tanned and healthy, and it made the white and blues of his clothes look brighter. Though shy under his gaze, she was thrilled by his attention; his words made her feel beautiful and alive.

Abigail knocked once on the door, then pulled it open. "Maybe later," she said coyly, before she could help herself. She looked away before he could answer and stepped inside.

The smell of her grandmother's cooking hit her instantly; after decades of her grandmother living and entertaining here, it remained in the air at all times, greeting Abigail upon her entrance like an old friend. She looked toward the back of the house, where sunlight poured in through the kitchen windows. The sound of bright conversation drew her forward, and she found her mother and grandmother seated at the round kitchen table, sipping tea.

"Hi, Mom," she said as she kissed her mother's cheek. "Good morning, Grandma," she added, bending to kiss her, as well. "You look fabulous today."

"Oh, I look all right," she said, tossing her hand in the air. She lifted her chin and smiled at her granddaughter. Her face was bright and beautiful, but thinner, showing her age; her voice was still cheerful, but it was shakier than it had been so many years before. She smoothed down the front of her pink ruffled blouse, and Abigail noticed how frail her fingers looked. "But you, my dear, are radiant." She turned to Gabriel. "It must be because you have this charming young man to escort you."

Abigail laughed. "I suppose it doesn't hurt."

"How are you, Mrs. Wheeler?" asked Gabriel. "I haven't seen you in a while."

"Not since fall," she said.

"Has it been that long?"

"I don't get out much anymore."

"Gabriel, have a seat," said the younger Mrs. Wheeler, Abigail's mother Eve. "I'll fetch you kids some lemonade."

Abigail and her mother brought lemonade and cookies to the table, and they all sat down. As they settled into their seats, Abigail took a moment to look around the kitchen she knew so well. It was an old farmhouse kitchen, with a white drainboard sink, painted white cabinets, and white and red gingham curtains tied back around the windows. A flowerpot with a tidy cluster of yellow flowers sat on the windowsill before each window. Spice racks filled with dried, fragrant spices dangled above the radiator. Various utensils hung from hooks beneath the cabinets. A dusty rug lay on the floor before the sink.

"So tell me, dear," said Abigail's grandmother. "What have you been doing since you returned home from school?"

Abigail brought her eyes to her grandmother once more and smiled. "I've been keeping busy. I've been to the soup kitchen, of course. I've been working at the bank. Also I've been reading a lot."

"Abigail wants to start a women's study group," Eve told her mother-in-law. "Isn't that a wonderful idea?"

"It's a lovely idea," agreed Mrs. Wheeler, "though it doesn't surprise me. Our Abigail is always doing great things, isn't she?"

"Yes, I'm very proud of her," said Eve, patting her daughter's hand. She was a pretty, sharp-looking woman with dark hair pulled back and pinned beneath an ivory pillbox hat. Her heart-shaped lips were painted red, and her jaw set firmly with her smile.

"Well, I will live vicariously through you, dear," said Mrs. Wheeler. "I wanted to go to college, myself. I considered taking a class or two after your grandfather died, but I never did."

"Why not?" asked Abigail.

"It was different for women back then. Besides, I had more important things to occupy my time."

"Like what?"

"Like you." Mrs. Wheeler laughed.

Abigail laughed, too. "That's very nice, but it makes me a little sad. I don't like that I was the reason you didn't fulfill a dream."

"Nonsense. I was perfectly happy dedicating my life to my family."

"I would have loved to go to college," said Eve. "If I had had my way, I would have studied astronomy."

Abigail stared at her. "I never knew that."

"Sure. The stars have always fascinated me."

"Why didn't you go to college?"

"My parents couldn't afford to give me an education. Then I worked as a secretary while your father was overseas. That's why

I'm proud for being able to send my own daughter to college." She smiled, and her pride was evident in her eyes as she gazed at her daughter. "You're the first woman in the family to go."

"What a wonderful honor," said Abigail, with a smile.

"I admire you, Mrs. Wheeler," Gabriel said suddenly, and everyone turned to him. "You sure were strong when Mr. Wheeler fought in France."

"Thank you," said Eve. Her eyes had turned misty but warm with appreciation. "I supported myself for a long time while waiting for Hank to return so we could get married and start a family."

"It must have been hard for you."

"It was very hard, as you know. Worrying about a loved one at war is terribly trying, isn't it?"

Gabriel nodded.

"I ache for your mother," said Abigail's grandmother. "There are no words to describe how I felt when Hank was deployed."

"It did bring us closer, though, didn't it, Rachel?" Eve said, patting her mother-in-law's hand.

"Indeed, it did."

Eve's smile grew more sober. She leaned back in her chair and folded her hands on the table. She turned to Gabriel. "It was the hardest time of my life. There's no denying that."

"I think you did a really good job."

"Thank you, Gabriel. That's nice of you to say."

Abigail looked between them and smiled, pleased.

The phone rang. Eve touched her mother-in-law's shoulder to indicate that she should remain seated, and rose to answer it.

Mrs. Wheeler turned to Abigail. "You'll find the strawberry patch is full of weeds, unfortunately. I can't tend to it like I used to."

"Your strawberry patch always has the biggest and the best strawberries," said Abigail kindly. "A few weeds won't change that."

Their banter was interrupted by the sound of crying. They all turned sharply. Abigail's mother was holding the phone to one ear; she held her face in the other hand.

Abigail and Gabriel stood.

Abigail's heart was racing; she felt its fluttering in her stomach. "Mom, what's wrong?" she asked, fearful of the response.

Her mother muttered a few words into the phone, then hung up, took a couple of shaky breaths, and rubbed her face with her hands.

"Danny Cutler was killed," she said.

Abigail's vision grew blurry, overcome by a hazy yellow light. She slumped back into her seat, staring at the floor with wide eyes as she pictured Rosie's face, only vaguely registering the sounds of women crying around her and the straightness of Gabriel's posture as he stood motionless beside her chair.

SHORTLY AFTER, Abigail and Gabriel sat in the strawberry patch in the backyard, but picking strawberries now seemed trivial and indulgent. They simply sat among the creeping vines, heavy with fruit that bent the stems toward the ground. The patch was thick with weeds and overgrowth, dozens of plump, overly ripe strawberries waiting to be picked, competing with the weeds for sunshine and rain.

Abigail had cried inside with her family and regained her composure before joining Gabriel in the yard. Gabriel had remained stoic.

"Poor Rosie," she said, nearly whispering as she held back tears. "I can't stop thinking about her. What should I do? Should I go over there?"

"No. Don't go now. Give them some time."

Abigail nodded. "Okay."

They sat in silence. Abigail watched the breeze rustle the

weedy strawberry patch. She glanced at Gabriel. He seemed lost in his own thoughts as he sat beside her, cross-legged and hunched over, picking at some crabgrass at his feet.

"You've been awfully quiet," she observed gently, placing her hand on his shoulder.

"I just feel sorry for the Cutlers."

She nodded again and said nothing. Her gaze drifting, she noticed out of the corner of her eye the movement of his arm as he pulled the clump of crabgrass from the parched soil.

"It's just such a waste, you know?" he added. "I mean Danny. Such a waste."

She nodded yet again, more slowly. "It truly is."

"I mean, he didn't even have a chance," he said. She turned toward him; his voice sounded more agitated. "He didn't have a chance to do anything with his life." He raised his arm and tossed the crabgrass far across the yard, into a thicket of woods. "Just such a waste."

Abigail opened her mouth to agree, but she didn't see the point; the situation was beyond words. She sighed and rubbed her eyes with her fingers.

"See, this is exactly what I was talking about," he went on. He shook his head, attacking another clump of crabgrass, the muscles of his shoulder and arm straining beneath the short sleeves of his shirt. "This is exactly what I meant when I said the world is a messed up place. You never know what's going to happen next. You go to war. Or you fall off a roof. Or a hundred other things." He paused for a moment, then shook his head and resumed his motions. "That's why I don't look at things through rose-colored glasses. Life is short. It's just so damn short."

Abigail didn't know what to say. His voice was growing more and more tense, and he had stung her with his comment about rose-colored glasses. She eyed him nervously, sensing he was more upset even than he was letting on.

He said, "I got drafted, Abby. They sent me the letter weeks ago."

Her heart seemed to sink like dead weight to the pit of her stomach; she felt suddenly cold, and she couldn't breathe. "What?" she cried after a moment had passed, now not believing him, and angry that he would lie to her. "You stop that! They did no such thing."

"They sure did. I report to the draft board next week."

"And you didn't say anything to me? You didn't tell me this was going on?"

"I didn't tell anybody, not even my mother. Especially not my mother."

"But..." She trailed off and shook her head. A thousand thoughts swirled through her mind, and she couldn't focus on any one of them. "But you have a brother there. They can't make you go, too, can they?"

"I guess we're going to find out."

As she recovered from the shock of the news, disbelief made way for terror. "What are you going to do?" she asked, trying to keep the desperation out of her voice.

He shrugged. "Nothing to do but meet with the board."

"Will you be able to get out of it?"

"I don't know. Maybe."

She studied him carefully, her eyes narrowing.

"Do you even want to get out of it?"

"I don't know, Abby," he said, turning to her now. His voice was harder and less patient, and she startled a little, taken aback. "I just don't know. There's a lot to consider."

"What is there to consider?" she said, not bothering to hide her emotion. "You have a life to live, with so much ahead of you. Your family already has a son there. You don't agree with the war. I just don't see—"

"That's just it, Abby," he stated, moving his hands up and down in a dramatic gesture. "My brother is there. He was brave.

He sucked it up and made those sacrifices. He met his responsibility. Am I going to be too selfish to do the same thing? Am I going to be too much of a coward?"

"Oh, Gabriel. You wouldn't be either of those things. You'd be meeting your responsibility to your family. You'd be courageous for standing up for what you believe in."

"I believe in doing the right thing."

She watched him as he turned back to the strawberries and picked at the grass before his feet. She was all at once almost tangibly aware of his size. She was hit in a flash by a memory, a distant vision from when they were children. It was hard to believe he was the same person, this strong, able adult with a house and a business, who spoke with such certainty.

"Do you want to go?"

"Of course I don't want to go!" he said. "Why the hell would I *want* to go? I'm no soldier. Furthest thing from it! I just want to live my life in my house and in my town, work my damn job, hike on the mountain when I feel like it and go home at the end of the day. The war is none of my damn business."

"Then that's what you should do, Gabriel. You're running your dad's business now, and Thomas can't work. Your family couldn't survive without you. You can get a deferment, I'd bet money on it. Don't let someone else make your choices for you. Make your own choices."

"The best thing I can do is get the most out of life while I can, while I'm still here. If I go, then at least I'd have lived to the fullest. At least I'd have given it my best shot."

Suddenly his eagerness to buy a house and settle down made sense. She recalled Patrick's words before deploying, that Gabriel live his life. She considered Gabriel's anxiousness and the tension with which he had spoken about the draft—and the fact that he apparently had already received his draft notice when he proposed to her. She wondered if he had proposed for this reason, if his desire to marry her was the result of his desperation to beat the clock. She knew he loved her, but she didn't know if his fear was clouding his judgment; she didn't know if he'd want to marry her this quickly under different circumstances. Before this moment, his proposal had seemed spontaneous and romantic. Now she felt distance between them, as if his goal was not to marry her but merely to marry, as if he was simply seeking the stability he thought marriage offered, as if any woman could have taken her place.

She felt disappointed and humiliated, like something had been taken away from her. She suffered a devastating ache in her chest, surprised by how deeply this possibility hurt her.

"You should do what you want," she said, a little coldly, and aware of it. "Don't feel pressured to make big decisions just for the sake of making them."

"I'm not doing that. Do you think I'm doing that?"

"I think getting married is a pretty big decision. Don't you?"

He turned to her, his brow furrowed. "What are you talking about?"

"Maybe that's why you're in such a rush to get married. I don't think it's on purpose. But I think it's possible." She was on the verge of tears; she breathed more deeply to hide it. She shrugged. "Just a thought."

He blanched, and his face turned to stone. He stared at her for a long time, then turned back to the strawberries, hunching over so she couldn't see his face.

"If that's what you think, Abby, you don't understand. You just don't understand at all."

She was growing more upset by the moment, what she perceived as the anger and condescension in his tone sharpening the pain and driving it even deeper. "Well, why don't you explain it to me?"

"Just forget it."

"No, tell me. I think you should tell me what I don't understand."

"I don't want to talk about it anymore. Forget it."

"But if you—"

"I said forget it."

Abigail's face hardened. She didn't know what to think or what to feel. All she knew was that things had changed. She sat back, chastising herself for chasing dreams like a lovestruck schoolgirl and for letting him hurt her feelings.

"Sorry," he said, his voice calmer now. He had turned his head toward her but did not look at her; his gaze was directed at the ground. "It's not your fault."

She softened tentatively. "It's okay. I understand."

His eyes met hers, but his face remained serious. He squinted against the sun, which seemed to sparkle like gold in his hair. "You do?"

He was himself again, and she felt sympathy for him. "Sure. You've been carrying this huge burden all by yourself." She frowned. "I feel terrible about that," she added, swallowing back tears.

He looked downward and sighed.

She rested her hand on his shoulder. "You do what you think you need to do," she said, though the words made her almost sick with fear. "Whatever that is."

He didn't look up, and he said nothing in reply. Instead, still sitting cross-legged beside her, he leaned in her direction, face toward the ground, until his forehead touched the side of her face. Flooded with relief, she wrapped her arm around his back and held him, his face in her neck and his hair now wet with her tears, tears that fell for so many reasons.

THEY STOOD, said a solemn goodbye to Abigail's mother and grandmother, and lumbered toward the sidewalk in front of the house. They stood there facing each other. Abigail was confused and anxious over their conversation, but she regretted that they had argued after his confession about his draft notice.

"I'm sorry," she said sincerely.

"No, I'm sorry."

They looked around, avoiding eye contact.

"You shouldn't be sorry," she said then, glancing up at him. "You have every right to be upset."

"Not with you, though."

Their mood was dark, and she didn't know what else to say. She rubbed her lips together, looking around.

"We didn't pick any strawberries," she said drily.

"Right," he said. He sounded tired. "Ah, well. It's not like the old days, I guess. We have real problems now, not like when we were kids."

"Oh, to be a kid," she said. "What a wonderful, innocent time that was."

"It sure was."

She sighed. "All right. I'd better go. I'm going to see Rosie tomorrow. I have to do something."

"Okay. Let me know how I can help."

They drifted toward each other and embraced as friends, as they always had. They held each other for many moments before reluctantly parting.

"I'll call you," he said, taking a few steps backward and lifting his hand for a casual wave.

She watched him for a moment as he walked down the street, this tall, straight-backed, complex man who had somehow materialized from the little boy she had known so well. With a heavy heart and a heavy mind, she turned and walked home, crying for Rosie, certain she would barely sleep a wink that night, and wondering if there was any meaning in the fact that she was going home without any strawberries for her pie.

～

"WHAT ARE YOU DOING NOW, LOVE?"

Abigail once again had the ingredients spread across the countertop, only this time the arrangement was messy, with the items assembled haphazardly, rather than in neat groups as they had been before. She also had laid out quite a few more ingredients than she had the first time. After visiting Rosie, she had returned to her grandmother's house to pick strawberries, and overflowing buckets of strawberries now sat everywhere—on the countertop, on the floor, on the chairs pulled out from the table. As she stared desperately at it all with Marion, it seemed the perfect representation of her state of mind: cluttered, disorganized, and frightfully overwhelming.

"I'm making a pie. I think."

"Another one?"

"Yes, another one."

"What happened to the last one?"

"It wasn't any good."

Marion was silent for a moment. "You've made that pie a hundred times."

"I know. I messed it up. I messed it up big time."

Marion said nothing. She looked around the room, eyebrows raised, and finally turned to Abigail once more.

"Seems like a lot of pressure just to make pie."

"It's important that I get it right. Maybe I'll give up. Maybe I don't even want the pie."

"It's just a pie, love."

"No, it's not just a pie! It's very important that I get this right. This pie is a big deal, and I just want to get it right. Is that so hard to believe? I know you're trying to help me, Marion, but please stop saying it's just a pie! It's so much more than pie! It's so much more!"

Abigail felt red in the face, and she was breathing hard. She ventured a glance at Marion. Marion was standing with her eyebrows raised and her mouth open. Her hand was outstretched; her magazine had fallen to the floor.

"Sorry," mumbled Abigail, turning toward the counter.

"It's okay," said Marion. "Do you want to tell me what the heck is going on?"

Abigail rubbed her lips together and faced her sister. She sighed. "I might as well tell you," she said. "You see, Gabriel asked me to marry him on Founder's Day, and we agreed I'd marry him if I won the pie contest. At first I was shocked, and then I was excited. But the more I think about it, the more I wonder if it's right for me. Do I want to settle down here, do I want to get married right away? I'm only 21. I'm still in school. Maybe I'd want to marry him in the future, but now? Maybe I should live my life now and settle down later. And what about that pie? Why the pie? Is it a sign? Is it an indication of things to come, a symbol of my future, baking pies? Because, you know, though Gabriel is forward in his thinking, he really is quite traditional. And speaking of which, the men here, oh Marion, did you hear them on Founder's Day? If Gabriel wants to stay here, what does that mean? And will I have to listen to those opinions forever? But on the other hand, will I ever find a more supportive husband than Gabriel? Haven't I always thought about him this way, hasn't it almost been meant to be? Do I want to push him away when I believe he can make me happy? And on top of everything else, he got his draft notice, Marion. The draft! It's so upsetting I can't even think about it. I just don't know what to do. I'm so conflicted, and I've never felt this unsure about anything in all my life..."

Her words trailed off as Marion approached her. She placed her hands on Abigail's shoulders. The two sisters locked eyes.

"Do you want to marry him?" Marion asked.

"It's not that simple."

"Why not? Forget about all that other stuff. Do you want to marry him?"

Abigail felt tears brimming and said nothing.

Marion said, "He loves you because you're you. The only question is, do you love him because he's him?"

As Marion picked her magazine up from the floor and walked from the room, Abigail felt herself relax. She closed her eyes, took a deep, calming breath, and made her mind clear. She felt the floor beneath her feet, the cool kitchen air on her arms, the force of gravity pressing on her from above. She opened her eyes and looked around at the kitchen of her childhood home. She noticed the bright yellows, reds, and oranges of the cheerful floral wallpaper, the canary yellow of the drawers, and the wooden cabinets. It was a space she knew well, in which she and her family had shared many happy times. She felt safe and restored once more.

She turned to the countertop and organized her ingredients. There were now three more manageable categories: essentials, like flour, sugar, and milk; her standards, like cinnamon and lemon juice; and other less usual ingredients she had taken from their places without knowing why, like cloves, cardamom, and rosemary. The first pie had been acceptable, but somehow she felt she couldn't enter the contest with the same old pie she had been making for years. She began scooping flour and sugar from their canisters and let her mind drift.

She decided to be honest with herself. She loved Gabriel, and she guessed she always had. It was almost as if they had known instinctively that they would end up together, and she wondered if this tacit understanding was the reason they had never talked about it before.

But it was one thing to dream and imagine, and another thing to actually do it. As she sliced the butter into even slabs and cut it into the flour mixture, she acknowledged that now that the reality was before her, she had to think it through, to analyze the details and make sure it was a dream worth realizing.

She combined the wet and dry ingredients, patted them into a ball, and rolled them out into a perfect, smooth circle. She carefully lifted the circle and pressed it into the bottom and sides of the dish until it had settled evenly into the shape of the crust. As she did so, she thought about how Gabriel appeared to be settling —into Linsbury, into marriage, into cynicism. He was letting events affect him to the point where he didn't believe there was hope, where he didn't think change was possible. She understood that his draft notice was darkening his perspective, and her heart ached for him. But she feared he was settling for a life he could have right away, because he was afraid—and if that was the case, it wasn't enough to justify this serious a decision. She was worth more than that.

She lifted a bucket of strawberries to the countertop and dumped them out so they scattered in all directions. She didn't doubt that he loved her. But he was so reticent at times; it was so hard to gauge how he truly felt. Undoubtedly he believed he wanted to marry her, but did he truly understand her, and if he didn't, would he still want to marry her if he did? She washed the strawberries, dried them, and hulled them, remembering with a sharp pang his suggestion that she looked at the world through rose-colored glasses. And though he had apologized, he wouldn't have said it if he didn't believe there was some truth to it. She didn't know if he would have chosen those words if he hadn't been so upset. All she knew was that she couldn't be with a man who thought she was naïve for seeing possibilities.

She sliced the strawberries down the middle with her knife and threw the pieces into a bowl. She rested her hands on the countertop and closed her eyes. She was determined to dictate the circumstances of her own life and not to settle—unlike her grandmother and her mother, who had not attended college, though they had wanted to. And in thinking about her mother, she let her thoughts drift to Gabriel's mother. For some time, she had suspected that Mrs. Kelly did not approve of her strong opinions and progressive ideas, and their conversation on Founder's Day had proven that she was right. She had deliberately withheld the details from Gabriel when they discussed it at the soup kitchen, but in her own kitchen now, she recalled the look on Mrs. Kelly's face upon hearing that she had considered going into government, the way she had raised her eyebrows and turned up her nose when Abigail had told her she planned to live by herself after graduating from college. Her own mother and grandmother had a loving, supportive relationship, and they supported her. Mrs. Kelly was stalwart and traditional, and Abigail was worried about what her relationship with her mother-in-law would be like.

She stared at the bowl of strawberry halves, wondering what to add next. She had made the same strawberry pie for years, but she knew it needed something different, something all her own. She picked spices and herbs from the counter, sniffing them and adding a sprinkle here and there, writing down what she was testing so she wouldn't forget. Her thoughts turned back to Gabriel. Her heart raced and dread filled her as she thought once again about his draft notice. She didn't think she'd ever forget the sound of his voice as he told her he had received it. She bit her lip, wondering if all these concerns were mere fronts for a greater, truer fear. He was her best friend, and she loved him. She was terrified he would be taken from her, especially now that a life with him was finally a real possibility. Maybe she was pushing him away to avoid the pain that would come from losing him, a pain that would last forever—was that possible?

Abigail didn't know the answer to any of these questions. She tossed the strawberry mixture to combine the ingredients, then dumped it into the baking dish and carefully laid the second circle of crust on top. As she pinched the edges and indented them all around with her fork, she realized she was no closer to making a decision than she had been before.

She sighed and shoved the pie into the oven, then set her kitchen timer and sat down to wait. She didn't see how this pie could possibly be any good when she had been so distracted as she made it. This pie had become much more important than she could have imagined, and she didn't know how to calm herself enough to do it well. It was something that should come naturally to her, and yet she was encountering so many obstacles. Perhaps this was a sign that she shouldn't be making the pie at all.

~

DEAR PATRICK,

I had a dream about you the other night. You and me and the others were sitting around a bonfire drinking beer. You were telling stories, and we were laughing. That was it, that was the whole dream. What makes it interesting is that I can remember just what your face looked like when you were talking. It was lit by the fire and was almost gold. You tilted your head back, remembering some happy time. I can still see your smile, even your teeth. You were wearing a plaid shirt and suspenders. I don't know why I remember that. It's funny, the things we remember about dreams.

I messed up with Abigail. She misunderstood me, and I over-reacted. The thing is, I thought I had been so clear. I thought I was pretty transparent. If I can be misunderstood even when I say it flat out, then what hope can I ever have?

With you being where you are and me maybe joining you one day, I can't care about anything at all, from important things like women to stupid things like my hair. Mom keeps telling me to cut my hair. I could cut my hair, but for what? What does it matter? It's empty, it's nothing. It's pointless. Little things like my hair. Messing around with any other women. Look around at the world. Who has time for them? They just don't matter.

Everything is changing, I don't know my role in it anymore. I don't even know my role in the family anymore.

My dreams about Abigail were the one stable thing in my life. I never expected them to come true. I was content to keep things safely as they were. Now she doubts I ever had them, and it feels like they're being taken away from me. And now that I've said it, I really want it. I wish I had never said anything at all.

Maybe it's for the best if it doesn't work out. I don't even know that she wants to stay here anyway. I'd probably only be holding her back. Maybe it was all just a fairy tale. The problem is, we're not kids anymore.

I've seen Abigail hanging out with other guys. I'm not going to lie to you. It scares me. The truth is, I've got very little experience with women. I wouldn't know what to do with a girlfriend even if I had one. Waiting for Abigail has made me ignorant of how to act or what to do, to the point where I wouldn't feel capable of making her happy anyway. The irony, it kills me.

In other news, Michael's baby can clap now. This is a very big deal. I haven't actually seen it yet because whenever they try to show us, she refuses to do it. You should see Mom with this baby. I've never seen Mom so happy as when she holds this baby. She says she loves having a girl around.

Pop still plays cards on Thursdays. I have to hand it to Mom. She takes really good care of him. She always makes sure he takes his medicine and does his exercises. That's one happy thing. I've been thinking a lot lately about Pop and Mom. I think we're pretty lucky.

About your last letter. We all smiled at your request for Chips Ahoy. Mom cried. Expect Chips Ahoy soon.

Your brother,
Gabriel

ABIGAIL RECEIVED a call from him a few days later. Marion answered the phone. She handed the phone to Abigail, whispered a lewd comment, snickered, and walked away, her nose in a magazine.

Gabriel apologized again for his outbursts at her grandmother's house and asked if they could start over. Abigail eagerly agreed that they should put it behind them. Relieved, he asked her if she would go hiking on the mountain with him that Sunday. He said she had taken him to a place where she felt small, but part of something, and that he wanted to do the same for her. Abigail accepted this invitation and hung up the phone with flutters in her chest. Spending the day with Gabriel on the mountain, just the two of them, would be romantic. However, she hadn't hiked the mountain in years. She was worried she would embarrass herself in front of Gabriel. In addition, she feared he would remind her about the strawberry pie. She still wasn't sure what she was going to do about that.

Saturday evening, she agonized over what to wear. She didn't have anything pretty that was also practical. She decided on knee-length denim shorts, and she borrowed Marion's sneakers. However, she wouldn't sacrifice her top. She settled on a white blouse with ruffles on the collar and sleeves.

He picked her up in his blue Chevy truck before the sun rose Sunday morning. The air was chilly, and as she settled into the seat, she shivered with cold and excitement. Exchanging some calm, friendly chatter, they drove through her neighborhood and up Main Street. The white two-story buildings that housed the post office, the barber, and the bank were still and silent.

Beyond the church at the end of the green, the road opened. The truck thumped as they crossed a red covered bridge that took them over the creek and onto a narrow, curvy road that wound its way through the trees. The woods cleared for a time, and her eyes followed the plump, elegant rolling of the hills to her right, square patches of farmland and wide stretches of forest in the foreground. Abigail had driven these streets many times but had never found them so beautiful. In the crisp, purple light of morning, the mist still heavy on the grass, the scenery looked magical, like a fairy land. Gazing out the passenger side window, she couldn't believe she had never noticed it before.

She stole a glance at Gabriel while she could still hide behind the fading darkness. She watched as the hills turned to white-peaked mountains, layers of blue in the cool dawn light. Then the sun peeked over the hills as they passed a vast open field filled with yellow wildflowers. The sky turned from purple to pink, and finally to gold.

When they arrived at the entrance to the hiking trail, the sunlight had turned cheerful. Gabriel parked in an alcove concealed by the trees. They emerged from the car and swung their arms into their backpacks. Abigail watched him shyly as he hitched his backpack onto his back. He was wearing a gray sweater and khaki-colored shorts, and hiking boots. He was all straight lines and angles. He pulled the straps tighter with quick, rough motions. Abigail noticed the curve of the muscles of his arms beneath his sweater.

He turned to her and smiled, holding out his hand. "Are you ready?"

Abigail stepped toward him and took his hand. Together they walked into the woods.

The trail first led them along the river, the edges of which were dotted with so many boulders that they reminded Abigail of a cobblestone street. The trees along the water's edge were like people, she thought, bowing their heads forward to observe their reflections. She laughed to herself and put these silly thoughts out of her mind.

They strolled at a leisurely pace until the incline became steeper, then marched with even steps up the mountain. The sun was higher in the sky now, and they began to sweat.

Abigail was eager to keep the mood light and to enjoy the day. "Why don't you tell me more about your house?" she said, between breaths. She was working hard, legs aching, but she felt healthy and alive, her heartbeat strong. "What made you buy it?"

"I don't know. I just wanted to do something. I wanted my

own life, to be serious. I know that doesn't make any sense. I really can't explain it."

"I think it makes perfect sense."

They walked on for some time. Abigail slipped on a rock, and he caught her. She experienced a tumbling sensation in her chest as his strong hand gripped her elbow.

"You'll have to show it to me," she said. "I can't believe you bought a house and I haven't even seen it yet."

"Come over any time," he said. "Just not Wednesday."

She felt knot in her throat. "Is that when you—"

"Yes."

She had so many questions, so many points she ached to make, but he clearly didn't want to talk about it, and she didn't want to push him. They walked on in silence. They came upon some obstacles, large boulders blocking the way, requiring them to step perilously close to the edge of the cliffs, and twisted patches of roots that threatened to trip them, sending them onto the rocks. Abigail was wary, but Gabriel helped her, reminding her to be careful and holding her when she stumbled. He knew where to go and how to step, and she depended on him, feeling vulnerable but safe with him as her guide. After a while, she enjoyed being led. There was a strange kind of comfort in it, being at the mercy of the mountain. Witnessing the complexity and magnitude of nature, she acknowledged that she was but one person with narrow experiences, that the world offered much for her to learn, much more than she ever could—and she recognized the beauty in this. She found herself thinking more and more about Gabriel, his instinctive knowledge of the land and how naturally he was in charge here. She saw him happy, free, and unburdened; she could almost see the difference in his gait as he marched with confidence through the forest. It was a different side to him, and a different side to her that was drawn to it. She liked that he had this power, and she liked that he had shown her a perspective she hadn't known before. It made her feel once again that the world had unlimited possibilities, that one never knew when a lesson was just around the corner. And she liked that she was understanding something new about herself.

But her thoughts continued to return to his draft letter, how the strength and skill he demonstrated on the mountain would mean only so much if he were sent to the war. She had trouble reconciling the contrast. She couldn't stop herself from imagining him injured, or worse. The vision was unbearable. She watched him as he trudged determinedly forward, his eyes focused. She yearned to embrace him, but refrained. She connected to him through conversation instead.

"Do you still hike a lot?" she asked.

"As much as I can."

"I haven't been hiking in years, not since before I left for school. I had forgotten how much fun it is."

The trail became quite narrow and the cliffs much steeper. They stepped closer toward each other and breathed more heavily as the climb grew more difficult.

"I couldn't go that long without the mountain. I need to get away from the town sometimes. Watch your step there," he warned, and waited for her to pass before him through a particularly narrow part of the path. He placed his hand on her back as she sidled through, helping her keep her balance.

"Do you come here by yourself?"

"Either by myself or with one of my brothers. Sometimes with my dad if he's up to it. Patrick used to come out here with me all the time."

Abigail placed her hand on his shoulder as they walked.

"He'll be home soon," she said.

"I hope so."

She patted his shoulder and retracted her hand. They walked in silence for a few moments.

"So you've never brought another girl here?" she asked then.

She shot him a coy smile, pretending to joke but curious to hear his answer.

"Why would I want to do that?"

"I don't know." She lost her momentum and backed down.

"I don't bring girls here," he said. "The whole point is to escape the bullshit."

"But you brought me."

Gabriel said nothing.

He inhaled deeply as they trudged up the mountain, exhaling as he looked upward into the trees.

"There are no other girls, Abby," he said finally. "Not in my life, not in the world." He turned, and his eyes met hers. She was taken aback, startled by the emotion there. She stepped backward, and stumbled over a rock; before she knew it, there was nothing but air beneath her, and she caught a glimpse of his terrified expression before tumbling over the tree-lined cliff.

She landed about six feet down, saved by a ledge jutting out from the cliff, with a tree curving toward the sun. Beneath her, the rocky ravine looked wild and threatening. She hugged her tree with gratitude, humiliated and scratched up badly, with a throbbing shoulder, but otherwise safe on the ledge.

"Abby!" Gabriel cried. Abigail summoned her bravery and looked upward toward the top of the cliff. He was leaning over the side, his eyes and mouth wide with horror. "Oh, my God! Are you okay?"

"Yes," she called back meekly.

"Are you hurt at all?"

"No," she answered, wanting to rub her shoulder, but afraid to.

"Can you reach my hand?"

She tried to move her hand but was incapacitated by fear.

"Don't move!" he said. "I'm coming to get you."

"Okay." She felt weak and powerless. She leaned her forehead against the tree and closed her eyes against gathering tears, mortified. "I'm sorry."

"Don't you dare apologize. Just sit tight until I can reach you. Okay?"

She nodded, her heart pounding and her stomach in knots.

She managed to look upward. He was assessing the outside of the cliff, trying to determine which way he should go. Finally he turned and faced the cliff, lowering himself gingerly and gripping the crevices in the rock with his fingers. Abigail was impressed. She couldn't believe the skill with which he tested the crevices with the tips of his boots, the understanding with which he used the texture of the rock to his advantage. She watched the underside of his boots grow closer, feeling safer and more hopeful all the time, not too frightened to notice the tight straining of his body as it expertly scaled the face of the cliff. When he was sufficiently close to the ledge, he dropped his feet down and stood beside her, pressed up close. He wrapped his arms around her and squeezed tight, breathing heavily.

"I thought you were gone," he said from above her, his head leaning on the top of hers. He rubbed her back with his hands, pressing her into him.

Abigail closed her eyes and breathed in, his sweat in her hair and the heat of his hands and arms around her waist and on her back. He was filthy and hot, and he smelled mossy like the mountain.

"Me too," she murmured. "Thank you for saving me."

"I could kick myself for letting you fall in the first place. If it hadn't been for this ledge, I'd have lost you."

"I'm very lucky," she said absentmindedly, still stunned.

"Shit," he laughed, releasing some tension. "I've never been so scared in my life."

"Me neither."

He pulled away. "Come on," he said. "Let's get off this tree."

He pressed her against the face of the cliff and maneuvered behind her until she was squeezed between them.

"I'm going to lift you up. Grab the edge when you can."

She nodded, terrified.

"It'll be okay. I've got you."

She nodded again. "Okay."

He gripped her waist tight; his fingers dug into her hips and sprawled along her back. He lowered his hands to her backside, pushing her upward and reconfiguring his fingers to make her more secure in his hands.

"Bring your right foot to that crevice," he called to her. "It's not that far. Then reach up and grab the edge of the cliff. You can do it, Abby."

She did as she was told. Her foot slipped once, and she gasped.

"That's okay. Try again. I've got you."

This time, she had learned from her mistake and wedged her foot more sturdily. She reached for the edge of the cliff. When she had taken hold, he pushed with his hands, and she easily pulled herself over.

"Good job! Way to go!"

She was jubilant, but she knew she couldn't relax just yet.

"How will you climb back up?"

"I've got it," he said, and hoisted his foot upward until it was lodged between the rock. As Abigail watched, tortured by the suspense, he swiftly climbed the wall, reemerging only a minute later and leaning forward with his hands on his calves, breathing hard.

Finally, he stood straight, looking dirty and ragged, but strong and healthy.

"Gabriel," she said. Tears sprang to her eyes; she could no longer hold them back. "Thank you. I'm still shaking. I can't believe what just happened."

He hugged her tight and kissed the top of her head. "No kidding," he said. "Just look at your hair." He fingered its disheveled tresses and smiled slyly. "It's a mess."

She brought her hands to her head and smoothed down her hair, steaming a little. "Is that all you have to say?"

"I like it au naturel. Since you asked."

She didn't know whether to be irritated or flattered. She looked at his face. It was dirty and sweaty, and it contrasted with the crystal blue clarity of his eyes.

"Well then," she said, trying to recover. "I'll have to fall off a cliff more often."

"You'd do that just for me?"

One corner of her mouth crept upward. "You're such a wiseguy."

"It's all an act. You haven't figured that out by now?"

They continued up the mountain. Abigail tried to hide her embarrassment and her fury with herself for being so vulnerable and needing to be saved. But as they neared the summit, emerging from the forest and onto a plateau of rocks covered with stubby shrubbery, Abigail forgot her trauma and her painful shoulder. She was overwhelmed by the beauty and grandeur of the scenery. All around her, the mountains cascaded into the distance, their peaks and valleys ebbing and flowing like great green waves. The air was different here, the silence more intense. With the horizon so far beneath them and only the sky above her, she felt she was at the top of the world.

He held her hand and led her toward the edge of the plateau. Sensing her worry, he stopped.

"Would you sit with me on that rock? Do you think you can?"

Abigail looked at the rock. There was nothing between the rock and the sky; it was the last place they could be on the mountain, without falling off the side. But she knew that the best views would be visible from that rock, that there was no point in coming all this way and missing out now. She knew he wouldn't put her in danger; she knew he would take care of her and that there was no one else in the world who could show her this view.

"Yes," she said. "I think I can."

They stepped toward the rock. His hand found her waist, and

they lowered themselves to sitting. They sat snuggled together, awed silent by the majesty of the Earth.

Abigail turned to him. He was observing the landscape solemnly, his eyes clear and blue as the sky. She watched him with wonder, amazed that he had gotten her on that rock, and with such gentleness. She never would have taken the risk herself; she never would have pushed herself this far, without his encouragement. Suddenly their experiences that day looked a lot less like her needing his help and more like his lifting her up, enabling her to help herself and to live more fully.

"I feel so small here, but it's a good small," he said then, seeming to read her thoughts. "It shows me what really matters, that there's so much more." He looked at her. "Do you know what I mean?"

"Yes," she said, sincerely. "It makes me feel like there are bigger things than our petty concerns."

He patted her hand a few times and held it for several minutes more. Finally they stood. They took one last look at the view from the summit, then turned and headed back down.

The descent was easier, and they talked freely. But the air was heavy with unsaid words. As they approached the river, the smooth round rocks interrupting the current, they paused to catch their breath and enjoy their last minutes on the mountain. They set up a picnic blanket and took a rest along the riverbank, then stood side by side along the river's edge, encased by the thick clusters of trees. Gabriel stood with one foot on the ground, one on a boulder, his hands on his hips as he cooled himself. Abigail's heart raced. She hadn't wanted him to mention the pie, but now she wished he would. He was looking out onto the water. He turned to her.

"You know, Abby. I've been thinking. I shouldn't have asked you to marry me. I'm sorry."

Her heart skipped a couple of beats, and she felt a sinking in her chest. She couldn't believe what she was hearing.

"What happened? Why have your feelings changed?"

"That's not what I meant," he said gently. "I meant that what's most important to me is that you're happy. And I don't want you to be with me because I pressured you. I want you to be with me because you want to be with me too."

She shut her lips tightly to control her breathing, and shook her head.

He said, "I see now that it was a childish dream. You have so much ahead of you, so much that you want and deserve. So I'm not going to bug you about it again. I promise."

Abigail didn't know what to say. She stood completely still and completely straight, contemplating these words and wondering how she could possibly respond, when suddenly he pulled his shirt off from the bottom, his torso stretching and his arms rising toward the sky, and threw it onto the ground behind him. He bent forward and stuck his hands into the water, and splashed it onto his face, chest, and shoulders.

Abigail stared at him in shock. Sprawled across his shoulder, wrapping itself over his rounded bicep and onto the straight plane of his back, was a tattoo. It was a bird, a falcon, its wings spread as if in flight. As he moved his arm, the bird seemed to move with him, and she watched it, mesmerized, unabashedly, until he paused in his motion, looking at her curiously.

"What is it?" he asked.

Abigail approached him. She kept going until she was just before him, standing with him on that cobblestone on the water. She brought her fingers to the tattoo and delicately brushed the tips across the curvy, elegant lines. He watched her with wonder, then bristled at the sensation of her fingers on his naked skin.

She looked up into his face, her body tingling. Through her half-closed eyes, she saw that his eyes were wide, unbelieving. She leaned in closer, inhaling his thick scent, mingled with dirt and sweat. She brought her hands to his chest. It was cold and wet from the frigid water of the river. She pressed her own chest to his, feeling the heat of his body through her now soaked blouse. She tilted her head upward, wrapping her hands around his neck so they were buried in his hair. He met her in a kiss with a long, low groan.

She opened her mouth for him and took in his tongue, savoring the saltiness of the sweat around his lips. She gripped him harder, her hands around the sharp angles of his jaw. He clutched her waist, and together they stumbled backward until they had fallen onto the blanket on the grass.

He lay on top of her, his hands in her hair, and she wrapped her legs around him, squeezing him tight. She took his hand in hers and placed it over her breast. He exhaled sharply.

She unbuttoned her blouse, exposing her crisp white bra. He stared at it, pausing to absorb every detail. He shook his head in reverence, slowly gliding his hands up and down her chest and belly as if he were worshipping them.

She watched him, stroking the side of his face with her fingers.

"I've imagined this a hundred times," she said boldly. "I don't mind telling you."

"Me too."

She waited for him to say more, or to do something, anything. But he said nothing and lay motionless, seemingly immobilized by the sight of her.

"What's wrong?" she asked.

He looked at her squarely. "I've never done this before," he said.

Her eyes opened wide. "You haven't?"

He shook his head. "No."

"What exactly haven't you done?"

"Any of it."

She smiled, her heart melting. "I love that I get to be your first," she said. "It means you'll always remember me."

"Like I need another reason to always remember you, Abby."

Her eyes softened. "Well, I've done it before. And I'm on the pill." She paused. "Is that okay with you?"

He nodded.

She eyed him curiously. "Does it bother you that you're not my first?"

He thought about this. "No, it doesn't bother me. Not for the reason you'd think."

"What do you mean?"

"Never mind. It's nothing."

Abigail had a hunch. "You know you're going to be great, right?"

He stared at her, his expression unreadable.

"Now what's wrong?"

"I'm trying to think of a wisecrack, but I'm coming up short."

"Then be serious," she said, nudging his hip with her thigh. "Is that it?"

"Could be."

She brought her hands to his face and smiled. "Gabriel," she said. "I really think it's time for you to stop worrying so much."

She pulled him close. He sighed out loud, his breathing turning heavy. They kissed a minute more, her hands running up and down his back and through his hair.

She let him undress her, pulling her arms back while he held the sleeves of her blouse. He was timid and nervous, and she encouraged him, whispering permission, taking joy in his fascination. His breaths were deep and ragged as his fingers touched and explored her. She watched his face as she unclasped his belt, delighted by the soft closing of his eyes.

They lay skin to skin. Abigail relaxed her legs and took him in her hand. He was warm and hard, and he throbbed beneath her fingers. She lifted her hips to meet him; he groaned again and stiffened, breathing heavily at her ear. She closed her eyes and took in the physicality of him—the weight of his body on hers, the curves and planes of his shoulders, back, and hips beneath her hands—and the thrill of knowing him now in this new way.

She pulled her hand away and arched her back, wordlessly guiding him; reading her signals, he lowered his hips, entering her with one swift, smooth stroke. Lips parted, she lifted her chin toward the open sky. With the sunlight filtering through the trees and the cool earth beneath her, the heat and comfort of his nearness, and the unreserved joy in his voice, she sighed aloud, having never felt more alive.

He was moving quickly and harshly, his rhythm messy, but beautiful. She gently directed him.

"Wait," she whispered, kissing the side of his face. "Don't rush."

He slowed himself, now stroking her face with his fingers and brushing his lips against the tender skin behind her ear. She moaned a little, pulling him close and bunching his hair in her hand.

In his excitement, his movements were erratic, but they grew steadier as he grew more understanding. Abigail gripped him tighter as she was carried away like the rushing water, and she prayed for him to regain some of his fervor. She indicated this to him with the quickening movements of her hips, and he sensed what she was asking of him, picking up speed and renewing his enthusiasm until she was as high as the mountain, the shuddering at her center washing through her. He immediately followed her, having intuited his need for patience and dutifully waiting, but barely. They kissed in the grass, sighing softly. She opened her eyes and looked into his, his face a silhouette against the sun.

They stood, stretched, and brushed themselves off. Naked, alone with him in the woods by the river, Abigail felt glorious, natural and free. She was looking out at the water, listening to its burbling as it rushed down the mountain and jumped over the rocks, when he scooped her up in his arms and carried her from the shore. Abigail screamed and laughed and fell with him into the chilly river.

Treading water, pushing her soaked hair out of her face, she shrieked and bristled with goosebumps, then laughed again as he dove under the water and goosed her from beneath.

They splashed and played around, tumbling together in the water, hanging onto each other and swimming upstream together, and letting the current carry them away.

Finally he took her waist in his hands and kissed her. He stood tall and firm in the water, the woods and the mountain the perfect background to his strong, bare form. She wrapped her legs around his hips and her fingers around the back of his neck. She kissed the bird on his shoulder, then met his eyes with her own.

"I will never forgive you for this, Gabriel Kelly."

"Please, punish me forever."

She leaned in and kissed him. He tasted earthy, like the river and the trees; his skin was cold, but his lips were warm and soft. His hands roved possessively over her, from her shoulders to her back, her breasts, belly, and hips. They were wet and smelled of the river, and she shivered where he touched her.

"Do you want to know why I had never been with anyone before?" he asked.

Her heart lurched. She nodded.

He took her face in his hands and kissed her lips once, gently. "It's because I've never loved anyone but you."

He kissed her again, more deeply. She felt weak, and she let him support her as he held her.

"I love you, Abby. Don't say it back. Just know that I do."

She let her chin lift and her lips drift toward his. She closed her eyes, neither seeing nor thinking, and reveled in the contrasts filling her senses—the babbling of the river and the quiet of the mountain, the calm of the forest and the beating of her heart, the frigidity of the river and the warmth of him.

ABIGAIL HAD WAITED until everyone in the house had turned in for bed. She didn't want any interruption tonight as she made what she hoped would be the final adjustments.

She stared at the ingredients on the countertop. Then steadily, with determination, she began baking a pie.

As she had a hundred times, she confidently combined ingredients and shaped her crust, this time without hesitation. She smiled. She couldn't stop thinking about the view from the top of the mountain. Even now, she still felt exhilarated, and she smiled when she imagined the impenetrable forests, the endless sky. She loved that she had been part of it and that Gabriel had taken her there. After years of her leading him, of his passively waiting for her to direct him, he had brought her to heights she never thought possible, and without any effort. It made their time together seem natural and right.

She admired the perfect heart-shaped strawberries as she tossed them with sugar. She wondered now what was so wrong with being saved. Why should she be frightened? When he saved her, she had also saved herself. Scaling the cliff, she had been strong enough to lift herself up and learn from her mistake before pulling herself to safety. The fact that he had held her steady should only endear him to her further—especially when she remembered that he had only ever supported her in everything she had ever done.

In fact, he had only ever followed her, with all her idealism and her stories; he seemed to crave them and to flourish with them, because they weren't something he could create himself. In this way she saved him, too. They needed each other. She chastised herself for thinking for even a moment that he didn't understand her. She knew her belief that anything was possible was the reason he loved her in the first place. And besides, their time together on the mountain had shown her how sincere he truly was.

As the pieces fell together in her mind, snippets of conversation made sense, and she felt she was finally seeing him for what he was. The fact was that he had a lot of responsibility at an age when other people were going to school or enjoying being young, living a life of newfound freedom. He was running his father's business, looking after Thomas, comforting his mother, and worrying about Patrick—all with the draft hanging over his head. Driven by his staunch morals and his desire to do the right thing, he had handled his responsibilities with dignity, even when his path had been determined for him—as she feared hers would be. And in spite of it all, he had made the most of it and created a life for himself, as much of his own life as he could.

She saw how much imagination he actually had. He saw possibilities in that little town, and he made it his own. She had always seen him as overly cautious and indecisive, content to go with the status quo—but now she recognized his vision, that he fought for what he wanted, that he was a risk taker, buying a house and running his father's business, and proposing to her after loving her all his life—which was more than she had done. He was brave for doing these things, not knowing what the outcome would be. In this way, he had been more courageous than she ever had.

In doing so, he had unwittingly shown her that she could, in fact, make her life whatever she wanted. There was no one mold, no one plan to which she had to adhere. She loved her town—her friends and family were there, and they were the reason she had returned. She shouldn't let a few provincial opinions scare her away if she wanted to be there. Times were changing everywhere, and she knew they would change there, too. She could handle Mrs. Kelly. By living a meaningful life, full of love and good deeds, she could prove to her that progress was nothing to be afraid of. She could shake things up as best she could, earn her promotion at the bank and study for business school, in the meantime helping people locally, where she was happy and comfortable. And besides, one couldn't find any place more beautiful than their little town by the mountain.

Whether he was drafted made no difference; it didn't change any of the wonderful things about him or anything she had learned about herself. It would only be a reason to hold him closer, to support him and cherish whatever time together they had. If he could be brave, so could she. She would be there for him no matter what.

With surprise she observed the crust-lined pie tin, just waiting to be filled, and the bowl of sugar-covered strawberries. She had been so deep in thought she hadn't even realized how much she had accomplished.

As for the pie, she knew what she had to do. She reached for a special ingredient, one her grandmother had never thought of, and smiled, her heart leaping. It was her grandmother's recipe, but she would update it for herself, making it her own. She would use the foundations she had been given, but would modernize it and make it new. As she sprinkled the sugar on top and slid the pie into the oven, she felt hopeful and unfettered. Being a "modern woman" meant she had choices, all choices. It didn't mean tradition was completely off the table; it meant only that she could choose the path that would enable her to celebrate herself, with a man who celebrated her, too. It meant she could climb the highest mountain or become president of the United States—or become meaningful in her own life and in her own town, and make a fabulous strawberry pie.

DEAR PATRICK,

You asked about the weather here. The weather has been beautiful, sunny but not too hot. Summer in Vermont is pretty great, I think. The days are warm but the evenings are chilly, and you can watch the sunset comfortably from the porch. I hope today the sun is shining for you and that you are safe for the moment, maybe smoking a cigarette as you read this.

Anyway. I want to tell you a story. A few months ago I was hiking the mountain. I was approaching the fork in the path by the boulder, and I turned toward the path on the right, as I usually do. But just as I turned my feet in that direction, a falcon landed on the path to the left. I stopped in my tracks and stared at it, and it stared at me. I don't know why, but I knew I had to hike that path. So to the left I went. I can't lie: I was nervous. I hadn't been up the path to the left in years. It's more treacherous, and I was by myself. I came to a spot and stopped again. There, in the woods, by the fallen tree with roots that look like a bear, was yet another falcon. Suddenly I remembered walking this path with you, years ago, and seeing a falcon in that exact same spot. I don't mind admitting it brought tears to my eyes. I watched the falcon for a couple of minutes before it flew away. Then I finished my hike, but I was so deep in thought I barely knew how I had done it.

That night I went into Darlingsburg and got a tattoo of that falcon on my shoulder. I wanted to remember how that falcon led me down the right path, for the second time. The guy who did it told me the falcon represents agility, independence, and personal freedom. That all sounds good to me.

I didn't say anything before because I thought it was sappy. I still think it is, but the difference is that now I don't care. Even since then I've somehow come to realize how important it is to say what you think, to be yourself. You never know what tomorrow will bring. And you may even make your life better.

That's all I want to tell you for now. It's just something I was thinking about. I'll write more soon, when I have more to say. I promise.

Your brother,
Gabriel

GABRIEL LEANED his head against the back of the rocking chair, enjoying the soft breeze that tempered the heat of the evening summer sun.

Though the weather was perfect, his neighborhood was still; his neighbors, most of whom had children, had walked into town for the little league game. Gabriel liked watching the kids playing on their lawns and in the street, but today he relished the quiet. He had met with the draft board that afternoon, and he needed to think in peace. The radio sat piping Frankie Valli in the corner of the porch. Every time the breeze whisked by, he closed his eyes.

It had been three days since he had been hiking with Abigail. Though they had talked briefly about what had happened on the mountain, shyly recalling details and smiling through the telephone, they hadn't discussed the obvious, how exactly their relationship had changed. Gabriel had been hopeful after they kissed goodbye on her doorstep that evening, finally allowing himself to believe it might have been meant to be. It had been the best day of his life, and he had thought she felt the same. But since then, her reluctance to reveal her feelings had made him once again realistic. He had been foolish to think he could sway her, and though he was disappointed, he wasn't dismayed. Mainly he blamed himself for placing this burden on their friendship, when he should have known it wouldn't work out. He forgave himself, though, content at least that he had made his best effort before letting her go. And in the meantime, she had shown him a beautiful new world and had given him a newfound confidence in himself.

He inhaled deeply, taking in the sweetness of the air. When he opened his eyes, a pale yellow Volkswagon was approaching, the driver searching for his house. Gabriel felt a pounding in his chest and a rush of relief through his veins. As she parked by the curb and stepped outside, holding a picnic basket, he stood slowly and smiled, careful not to appear as elated as he was.

"Hello, Gabriel," she said from the walkway. She was wearing a cheerful A-line dress that pleated all around and belted at the waist. It was sleeveless, boasting a deep v-neck, cornflower blue in color and dotted with little yellow flowers. A yellow kerchief covered the top of her head and tied in a knot at the base of her neck, but her hair was hanging free, its wavy tresses trailing behind her as she walked. She smiled at him as she gingerly climbed the steps and met him on his porch. It was a subtle but warm smile. Her lips were painted pink, and with their fullness and the way she had them tightly shut Gabriel was reminded once again of strawberries.

They stood facing each other on the porch.

"I thought I'd pop on over to see your house," she told him. "And also to let you try my pie."

She raised her arm, indicating the basket. He took a breath, trying to feign calmness. The suspense was unbearable. He didn't know if this was an answer, or just a pie, but he was determined not to ask.

"I'm glad you did," he said casually, his eyes crinkling in the corners, "though I'm afraid it's not much of a house."

"Oh, it's a wonderful house."

"It needs a lot of work," he said, glancing around at the chipping blue-green paint and the rickety steps. "Not exactly a dream house."

"Don't be silly. Of course it is. I love this porch," Abigail said. She looked around, her eyes wide, first at the ceiling of narrow wooden planks, then at the thick molding that met the painted beams, then at the spindles that lined the edges, then at the hardwood floors. "What a charming spot. I'll bet you sit out here all the time."

"I do," he said, looking around himself. He dabbed at the floor with his foot. "As you can see, the paint's in terrible condition, and half the planks are popping up. Patrick's going to help me fix it up when he comes home. But it'll do for now."

They said nothing for a few moments.

"So," she said, with a crooked smile, looking at him out of the corner of her eye. She reached inside the basket and retrieved a strawberry pie. "It's the moment of truth."

A little grin crossed his lips. "Have a seat," he said.

They sat beside each other on the porch. Abigail withdrew two plates, two forks, and a knife, then slid a slice of pie onto each plate.

He took the plate she offered and looked at the neat, dainty triangle. He broke a piece off with his fork and took a bite, working hard to suppress his grin at the taste of the sweet, supple fruit and flaky buttery crust. His heart beating faster, he cleared his throat in an attempt to appear unmoved.

"What's your feeling?" he asked, avoiding her gaze as he dug his fork in for a second bite.

"I have to admit that I'm really rather proud of it."

He was silent once more, using the pretense of chewing to avoid saying too much. He composed himself and swallowed, then favored her with a smile.

"You've outdone yourself, Abby. You'll win that contest for sure."

"If I do say so myself, I think you may be right."

"What's in it?" he asked curiously, digging in for another bite. "There's something different here, but I can't place it."

"It's fresh sage from my little window garden. I wanted something earthy to complement the sweetness. I took a risk. It paid off."

"Sure did."

He collected the plates and placed them on a table next to his chair, then stood and held out his hand.

"Come on inside," he said. "Let me show you around."

They walked into the house, their footsteps echoing in the

hallway, which was empty except for a ladder, some paint cans, and a variety of tools. The rooms were nearly empty, as well, but they were spacious and bright, with wide bay windows and cozy nooks and crannies. Abigail's head turned this way and that, admiring the high ceilings and hardwood floors. She walked into the living room and peered over the radiator out to the porch, then into the kitchen, with its beige linoleum floor and red and white wallpaper. Running her hand along the bannister of the tall staircase as she strolled by, she stepped into a sunroom in the back of the house and stopped to watch a bunny hop through the ample backyard.

Gabriel joined her in the sunroom and stood with her, his eyes on the placid scene.

"Bedrooms and bathrooms are upstairs," he said. "There's a nice work shed for me in the back. Decent sized attic, too."

She nodded, her gaze still outside. Gabriel waited for her to say something. Finally she turned to him.

"I guess you must know why I'm really here," she said.

Gabriel said nothing, watching her with his heart thumping.

She studied him for a moment or two. Then her expression softened, and her eyes grew misty. "I'm just going to come right out and say it. I've kept it from you for too many years." To hold back tears, she frowned, her strawberry lips turning downward prettily. "The truth is, I love you. And I always have, ever since we were kids."

He was still, save for the rising and falling of his chest. He furrowed his eyebrows as he registered what she had said. "But... Why didn't you..."

"Why didn't you?"

Dumbstruck, he listened in silence.

She said, "When you never said anything, I thought I was unrealistic to think that you'd ever love me as anything more than a friend. Then when you confessed your feelings, when being together became a possibility, I worried too much over silly things that aren't important enough for me to talk about now. But of course I loved you. How could I not?"

He frowned. Suddenly everything was different. The years played back in his head like a movie as he recognized how much time he had wasted with worry.

He said, "I thought I was the one who was unrealistic. I thought you wanted more."

"What else is there? I want to make something of my life, yes. But I want to be happy, too. And being with you would make me happy."

He felt his face contract with emotion, his heart pounding. He swallowed.

"I'll enter the contest," she said. "But I really don't care if I win." She frowned against tears. "I'd like to ask," she concluded shakily, "if you'd marry me."

He grew more alert, beginning to emerge from his disbelief. "You're asking me to marry you?" he said, his chest flooding with joy as he understood that this was really happening, that it wasn't a dream. "Are you kidding?"

They embraced, holding each other for a long time before sniffling and separating, gazing at each other tearfully.

"There's a catch," she said. "I want to finish college. We can get married before or after I finish. But that's important to me."

"That's not a catch, Abby. I want you to finish. And I'll wait for you. Hell, I've been waiting for twenty-one years."

She smiled brightly. "Okay then. That's settled. Thank you." Her smile dimmed then, and she bit her lip. "One more thing," she said, making an effort to firm up her expression. "About your draft notice."

"Actually, I—"

"No, hold on. I need to say this." She took a deep breath and looked at him closely. "You need to do what you feel is right. Of course I don't want you to go." She paused here to swallow back tears. She squared her jaw and made her voice steady. "But I understand if that's your decision, and I'll wait for you."

"I appreciate that, Abby. More than I can say." His eyes crinkled as he kept a smile at bay. "But I got a deferment." He reached into his pocket and removed a folded up piece of paper. He held it between his fingers and grinned. "They made the decision right there."

"Oh, thank God," she cried, and burst into tears. She sniffled and wiped her eyes with the backs of her hands, her chest rising and falling as she sobbed uncontrollably. He rubbed her back with both hands as he waited for her to calm herself, moved by her reaction.

Finally she looked up at him with red, glassy eyes. "I know you were ambivalent, and I was prepared to support you no matter what. But I have to tell you, I was terrified." She sniffled again, then smiled. "Are you okay with it? Do you feel good about it?"

"Yes," he said. "I wanted to do the right thing, but I've come to terms with what I think that is. My family needs me here."

"Yes, they do. And so do I."

He pulled her close again. She rested her head on his chest, and he kissed the top of her head. He sighed and closed his eyes, having never felt this happy and at peace in his life.

"I can't believe you doubted I could feel that way about you," he said, shaking his head. "I always thought you were perfect."

"Even though I wear rose-colored glasses?" she asked with a laugh.

His face turned grim, and his chest ached. "I shouldn't have said that," he said. "I'm so sorry."

She lifted her head from his chest and looked at him. "Don't worry about it. Really. You were upset."

"That doesn't make it okay." He felt his face flush, furious with himself for hurting her feelings and for putting a strain on their relationship before it even started. "I wish I could go back in time and take it back."

"You know what, though? You were right." His arms still around her back, she brought her hands to his chest and fiddled with the collar of his shirt, avoiding his gaze. "I should have given you more slack. You have every right to feel disillusioned." She met his eyes now and brushed his jawline with her fingertips. "I've been trying to work up the nerve to tell you that."

"Don't give me more slack. Wear your rose-colored glasses. Please." He was feeling overwhelmed once more, his skin tingling under the light touch of her fingers. He rubbed her shoulders with his hands, his eyes turning tender. "Abby, your optimism is the only thing that keeps me going sometimes. It's what I love most about you."

She smiled. "I know. Thank you."

He continued watching her. "I have to confess something," he said, still overcome. He blinked a couple of times and squared his shoulders, then smiled. "I had you in mind when I bought this house. I bought it for you. It was just a dream, of course. I never thought it would actually happen. But look at this."

He took her hand and led her through the sunroom and into the sunny backyard. He pointed her toward the left, where a large garden sat overgrown in the light.

"Strawberries!" she cried, clasping her hands together with glee. "Did you plant them yourself?"

"Absolutely not. That's your department. They were here when I arrived."

"Why didn't you offer to let me use them for the pie?"

"I didn't want to mention that damned pie. I had already made you uncomfortable enough."

"It's my turn to confess," she said, gliding her hands over his chest and shoulders, making his breath deepen and his heart race, and clasping her fingers together at the back of his neck. "I've been baking strawberry pie for years, but for some reason, I couldn't get it right. I wanted it to be special." She smiled sweetly. "I suppose I wanted to make sure it was good enough to win."

"I never doubted you could do it. Strawberry pie is your specialty. That's why I said it."

"And I'm so glad you did."

She lifted her chin and closed her eyes. He leaned in and kissed her, the act instinctive and natural, as if it had always been. He felt he would burst with happiness.

"So how did you think I would respond?" she asked brightly as she pulled away, her smile widening. "Were you expecting me to say yes?"

He shrugged. "I don't really know what I expected. I was just rolling with it. I'll tell you what I *didn't* expect, and that's for you to track me down and beg me to marry you."

She clicked her tongue and shook her head, but her eyes were playful. "I didn't beg. And you're never going to let me live that down, are you?"

"Probably not."

He took her face in his hands and kissed her, then pulled away and sighed.

She looked up into his face, leaning her head back and letting him support her as he held her. "That's fine," she said, smiling as brightly as the sun that made her hair a honey gold. "Maybe it will remind you that you do measure up, that you can do anything."

"I know that's true," he said, overcome once more, "because I have you."

She lost her breath a little, her lips parting, and he knew that moment would stay with him forever. He leaned forward, catching a glimpse of her closing eyes and rising chin before he met her lips with his own. Standing there in their backyard, the sun in his hair and the love of his life in his arms, he couldn't believe it was real, that he had achieved everything he wanted. It was Abigail, his Abigail, the same Abigail he knew, but so much more. He breathed her in, and she filled him, and he knew more than ever that he was home.

Dear Patrick,

I made Mom promise to let me be the one to tell you. I got engaged to Abigail. That's right, she said yes. Hell yeah, she did. She said it before she even won the contest. We want to get married right away, but we're going to wait for you to come home. And there's nothing you can say to make us change our minds.

But before that happens, she has to go finish her last year of school. That'll be hard. I can wait, though. At least I can drive down to see her on weekends, and she can come back to see me, too. She says to look on the bright side, that time apart will only make us happier to get back together. I could do without the time apart, but it's hard for me to argue with her, about that or anything else. Abigail says she can't imagine a better life for herself and that she's glad I was brave enough to ask her to marry me. I just can't argue with anything that she says.

She is going to move in with me before then, though. Whenever she comes home from school, she'll just come back here. Marion is moving out when she gets married in the fall, and Abigail feels it's time for her to leave, too. And anyway, as Abigail says, it's 1967, and times change. Mom doesn't change, though. As you can imagine, she's not happy about this. She says it's scandalous and that we'll be the talk of the town, that we'll embarrass her and our families. I feel bad about making her upset, but I'll be damned if I'm just too happy to care. Abigail living in my house? Yes, please. As soon as possible.

In the meantime, I won't be sorry to see the town empty out again when everyone else goes back to school. This is where Abby and I differ. She likes the protests, she likes the action. She likes to engage in conversations about the war. But it only makes me mad. Mad at the war, mad at the government, mad at the people who disrespect you when you come home. I can disagree with the war in private, without all that. I'd rather bring those thoughts to the mountain, where I can see the big picture, where I know it'll be okay.

There's something else. I was called for the draft, but I got a deferment. I feel a lot of guilt over this, but mostly I feel relief. I'm sorry, Patrick. I hope you don't think I've betrayed you. But this way I can make sure the family is okay. My consolation is that you will be home soon and all will be well again. I just know it.

I want you to be my best man. There's no one else who can do it, so you need to make sure you come home.

Honored to be your brother,

Gabriel

THE END

THE KELLY FAMILY

She's created the perfect life. But when it doesn't turn out as planned, can she take what she's learned and find her way in the darkness?

Meredith Beck had it all: the love of her life, a thriving career, and an apartment in the excitement of New York City. Then tragedy strikes, leaving her adrift in a world that's suddenly lost its luster. Optimistic by nature, she desperately attempts to rebuild. But no matter how hard she tries, she just can't muster her former strength.

Then a light appears in the darkness: Nick Kelly, a quiet painter from a small town in Maine. Thoughtful and kind, and utterly without pretension, Nick is unlike anyone Meredith has ever known. She is drawn to his love of nature and is comforted by his purity of heart. Through his eyes, the world seems to hold limitless possibility, and as their romance blossoms, she's delighted to find herself on the road toward a simpler life, with a partner who reminds her of the beauty in every moment.

But it isn't as simple as it seems. As Nick's own demons surface, the life they're building threatens to unravel. Human fallibilities once again complicate best-laid plans. And it becomes clear that before they can embrace the future, they must confront the lingering ghosts of their pasts.

A story of love, loss and the power of second chances, *Meredith Out of the Darkness* is first in a slow-burn series of cliffhangers ending with a warm and satisfying happily-ever-after.

ALSO BY AMANDA GALE

Meredith out of the Darkness

Meredith Against the Wind

Meredith Into the Fire

Meredith With the Waves

Love in the Lavender

Sweet Lavvy

Catherine and the Wind

Gwyneth in the Garden

Maeve in the Morning

The Magic You Bring

Dahlia Almost Drowning

ACKNOWLEDGMENTS

Thank you to readers Jessica, Cindy, Kristen, Teresa, Sarah, G. G., Elizabeth, Tellulah, Constance, Tammy, George, Melissa, and Erica. Thank you to Megan and Jane for helping with the finishing touches.

Thank you to my parents for discussing the 1960s and to Kaylee and Missi, who shared their perspectives about the experiences of military families. Thank you to Jen, who spoke with me about her father Bruce Patterson, a Marine and Vietnam veteran. A special thank you to John Shea and Hank Povinelli, who were kind enough to discuss with me their experiences in Vietnam, as well as their honest thoughts looking back on that time. I am grateful for the knowledge I've gained, and I hope this novella reflects my respect.

Thank you once again to Dez, who knows my characters as well as I do, who sees every stage and every draft, and whose patience with me is unending.